Cou
(A Netball
By Deb McEwan

Cover Design by Jessica Bell

The Positions

From the International Federation of Netball Associations

Playing positions and their roles on the court - There are seven playing positions in a team. Each has an important role to play for their team

Goal Shooter	To score goals and to work in and around the circle withthe GA
Goal Attack	To feed and work with GS and to score goals
Wing Attack	To feed the circle players giving them shooting opportunities
Centre	To take the centre pass and to link the defence and the attack
Wing Defence	To look for interceptions and prevent the WA from feeding the circle
Goal Defence	To win the ball and reduce the effectiveness of the GA
Goal Keeper	To work with the GD and to prevent the GA/GS from scoring goals

The Main Players

Goal Keeper	Rose/Marsha
Goal Defence	Kaitlyn/Rose/Sandy
Wing Defence	Sandy
Centre	Sasha/Kaitlyn/Chardonnay
Wing Attack	Suzanne/Sasha/Chardonnay
Goal Attack	Carol/Suzanne
Goal Shooter	Penny/Suzanne

Supporting Cast

Keith	Marsha's husband
Paul	Penny's husband and Kaitlyn's father
Brian	Paul's advisor and friend
Ann	Marsha's mother-in-law
Sam	Carol's husband
Leon	Sandy's husband
Natalie	Opposing team Goal Attack/Goal Shooter
Liz	Natalie's Mum – Goal Attack/Goal Shooter
Cathy	Plays for the Jaguars
Jo	Plays for the Jaguars
Amanda	A player in Spain
Melanie	A player in Spain
Kai	Entertainment's Manager (and more)
Derek	Investigator
Gary	Works on the base
Lynne	League Chairwoman
Gail	Non-playing umpire and Deputy Head of the league
Grace	The Eagles Centre
Mike & Hazel	Suzanne and Chardonnay's parents

Netball - A game with seven players on a side, similar to basketball except that a player receiving the ball must stand still until they have passed it to another player.

But it's so much more...

Chapter 1

Carol parked the car and smiled at Marsha. She grabbed her bag out of the back and nudged her friend into action. Marsha took a deep breath and followed Carol into the sports hall. She hadn't been in a gym since high school and this was nothing like the ones she remembered as a kid. Various courts were marked out in different coloured paint and the floor was so large that curtains were at the half way mark so different sports could be played at the same time. She looked up to the balcony where a number of people were training on treadmills – *great. People to laugh at me while I make an arse of myself.* Marsha hadn't played netball since school. In fact, discovering she was pregnant on her fourteenth birthday had put paid to any aspirations to play netball or anything else for that matter. She bottled it. Carol saw her plan before she could execute it.

'Hey, Rose.' Rose and the three women she was talking to turned to Carol. 'Remember Marsha? She's decided to give netball a shot.'

Rose was the scary woman who'd interviewed Marsha. She nodded hello. While one of the other women sized her up, Marsha wondered if a shoelace was undone or if she had rogue snot hanging from her nose, the inspection was so intense.

'Hi, Marsha. How's the job?' asked Sasha, the other woman who had interviewed her.

'Yeah, great thanks. It's good to get out of the house.'

'We'll talk later,' said Rose. 'Chardonnay,' she shouted to a teenager who was talking to two other youngsters. 'Do the warm up.' Chardonnay rolled her eyes to the other two but moved nonetheless.

'Come on then, ladies. Let's get going.' Most of the other women and girls followed Chardonnay and they started a slow jog around the gym. Penny, the woman who had sized Marsha up, held back with Rose.

'I wonder where she does her shopping?' she asked.

'It's certainly not House of Fraser, Penny, but I'm sure it won't affect her netball ability, that's if she's got any.' Rose did a quick leg stretch. 'Come on, let's join the others.'

As the group ran past, Marsha noticed Suzanne who pulled a face at her, then leaned towards the girl she was running with and whispered in her ear. They both turned, looked at Marsha and laughed. She reddened, trying her best not to let Suzanne wind her up. She was so out of her comfort zone and knew it wasn't going to be easy. As well as being a newbie she felt massive amongst the majority of the players. The few women who were bigger looked toned and Marsha felt like a baby elephant. *One small step at a time* she kept reminding herself but it wasn't working.

'Carol, make sure the balls are pumped up for the drills,' said Rose. 'Ah Sandy, nice of you to join us,' she called to the Fijian as she entered the hall, late as usual. 'Did you get dressed in the dark?' Marsha cringed for Sandy who was wearing tight purple leggings and a bright orange t-shirt. The loud colours suited her and she could quite happily have throttled Rose first then Suzanne, in another universe where she wasn't too frightened to speak up for herself and others. Sandy was a similar size and this, along with her warm smile, made Marsha feel a lot better.

'Are you waiting for something?' Rose looked at Marsha who said nothing.

'Well come on then, go follow what Chardonnay does to get your muscles warm. We don't want you injuring yourself on your first session.' Marsha obeyed but knew she wouldn't be back the following week if the others were as rude as Rose or as snide as Suzanne. Her head was all over the place from meeting so many new people, and she worried she wouldn't be able to remember their names.

Fifteen minutes later she was hanging out of her arse. Now she knew what the expression meant after overhearing it at work the previous day. Quite pleased she was able to keep up with the others at first, Chardonnay then decided to push her. She thought that running up and down the hall swinging arms, lifting knees or kicking her bum with her heels wasn't her idea of a good time but Marsha was enjoying herself, if she forgot about the fact that she could hardly breathe. She felt alive and although Rose was rude and bossy she was having a laugh with those she thought of as the normal women and girls. She also forgot about whether the people on the treadmills were watching. When they took a drink break Rose interrupted Carol and Marsha's conversation.

'So when did you last play?'

'In high school, but only up to age thirteen.'

'What happened to make you stop?'

Marsha clammed up. Her past was her business, but Rose caught her on the hop and she couldn't think of a reason to stop playing at that age. Carol came to her rescue.

'What position did you play, Marsha?'

'Centre. I was quite fast in those days…'

'You're kidding right?' Rose laughed. 'You're too big for Centre. You look like you'd make a decent keeper or shooter,' she threw a Goal Keeper bib at Marsha. 'See how you get on there. Carol and Sandy will show you what's expected while the rest of us do some drills.

'But, I quite liked Centre.' She was embarrassed that Rose had called her big but didn't know how to respond. It didn't matter as her comment fell on deaf ears. Carol gave her a sympathetic look, grabbed a ball and they made their way to the shooting circle. Yet again, it was well outside Marsha's comfort zone.

Chapter 2
Six Months Earlier

Keith was late coming home, later than usual. Sick of waiting, Marsha went to bed. It was already too late to eat for a normal person but her husband often got the munchies after a skinful. Surely he'd be able to heat up the Bolognese if he was that hungry? Deep down she knew he was capable of setting the house on fire when drunk. This kept her from sleeping soundly. She must have dozed off but the scratching at the front door woke her. The red light on the clock read 2.19 am. She put on her dressing gown and rushed down the stairs. Taking a deep breath she wondered which version of her drunken husband would be on the other side of the door. She pulled it open then moved out of the way as he fell into the hallway.

'Hello, darling.' Keith staggered to his feet and gave Marsha a wonky smile. She sighed with relief and gave a false smile, he wouldn't notice in his condition. This version of drunken Keith was a fool, but generally a happy fool and more like the man she thought she'd married. The other version was one to avoid at all costs. She rubbed her cheek subconsciously, recalling the punch she'd been too slow to avoid the last time he'd been drunk.

'Make us an egg banjo.'

'You're a bit late.' She was careful to make it a statement and not an accusation. He could turn from happy to angry at the flick of a switch.

He frowned. 'The steel works is closing. Pished because we're all losing our jobs. What's the point.' He bounced off the walls into the sitting room and crashed on the sofa. That'll be one of the first things to go she thought, relieved that he'd fallen asleep. He'd be gagging for a drink when he woke up so she went to the kitchen and returned with a glass of water. She placed it on the coffee table, far enough away so he wouldn't knock it over if he turned in his sleep. Putting a blanket on him she left him to it.

So the conversation she'd heard at the supermarket checkout wasn't a rumour. She wondered how long he'd known. Marsha's legs felt much heavier as she walked upstairs, pondering how they'd manage and not looking forward to the future one little bit.

*****

The Steel Works closed and he'd lost his job. Life had been bearable three months earlier but not now. It was Saturday night. Marsha was in with her mother-in-law and Keith was down the pub. As her mind wandered, she remembered when they first decided to move. Fair play to Keith who had protected her from the full wrath of her mother-in-law. He said that Ann had played hell. She blamed Marsha and accused her of stealing her son. He'd said his mother had ignored the fact he had secured a job in the Steel Works that would give them a reasonable standard of living. Marsha wanted to work but he'd put his foot down, insisting that her job was to make their house a home. They'd agreed that Ann would visit every other month and stay overnight. It was always the longest day for Marsha but she managed to keep her thoughts to herself in order to keep the peace. She'd tried to be friends and did her best to like her mother-in-law, to no avail. Ann disliked her and put her down at every opportunity. She wasn't even allowed to go to her house and if Keith visited, he went alone. Over the years Marsha found it more difficult to keep quiet and had invented the odd migraine in order to escape and stay sane.

She looked at her now. A short woman best described as buxom. She had an attractive face, but her forehead was set into a permanent frown. She loved watching *The Chase* and Marsha felt the walls closing in as her mother-in-law watched the repeats from the previous week on catch up. It wasn't as if she went anywhere during the week to miss the programme, she just preferred watching it while the sports stuff was on the other side during Saturday evenings.

'Look at the state of them,' her knitting needles continued their clickety clacking as she criticised the contestants on the programme. They turned as the front door opened signalling Keith's return from the pub. The one good thing when Ann visited was that Keith was on his best behaviour and wouldn't have dreamed of returning home drunk.

'Hello, son. Look at this one eh,' she nodded to the contestant on the TV. 'They should call him Chubby Chase. Get it?' she chuckled and Keith joined in. Years before Marsha would have laughed out of politeness, but not now. She wondered what she'd done to deserve this life then tried to sweep away the guilty

5

thought. The contestants were overweight, but so were they, a fact that Ann had chosen to forget.

'Go on, Marsha, laugh. Your face won't really crack you know,' she turned to her son and mouthed 'miserable cow.' Keith and Ann laughed again.

'I'm sorry but I'm not feeling very well. I'm going for a lie down.'

'What about my tea?' asked Keith.

'It's in the oven.' *Yeah, thanks for your support Keith.*

'She's always ill that one. You need to sort her out, boy.'

Marsha heard her mother-in-law's words. She'd heard worse and felt like she had the weight of the world on her shoulders as she trudged wearily up the stairs.

*****

On Wednesday the following week the bombshell dropped. It came in the form of a call from the bank and the woman asked to speak to Keith. He managed all the finances and they didn't have a joint bank account. The house and mortgage was in both their names so the bank clerk advised Marsha that if the mortgage arrears weren't paid by the end of the month, the house would have to be put up for sale.

'You can't call today and tell me we only have ten days. There must be some sort of law against that.'

'Mrs Lawson, your husband has been advised of this twice. The last time when he was in the bank,' Marsha heard her flicking through her papers, 'on Monday. We gave him some paperwork for you to sign and he said he'd return it to us when you got home from hospital.'

So he'd kept her in the dark by making up a lie, the devious git. She knew how convincing and charming he could be when he wanted something so she didn't blame the bank. She tried her best not to take her frustration out on the woman.

'And if my husband was lying, does that mean you can give us more time?'

'Can you come into the bank, Mrs Lawson? I can show you exactly where we stand.'

They hung up and Marsha readied herself. She dressed in her only decent skirt and blouse. Knowing she had a fight on her hands she at least wanted to look smart.

Weak sunshine shone through the clouds brightening up the high street. In the three months since the Steel Works had

6

closed businesses had gone bust, and shops were already boarded up. Marsha noticed nothing. In her mind everything was a dull grey and she couldn't see beyond it. They owed too much and the only way to repay it was to sell the house. Keith had been spending more than he earned and had taken out a bank loan. No savings meant no hope and even worse, if the house wasn't sold within a month, it would be repossessed. She should have felt pleased at securing them an extra month but all she felt was total and utter despair. The one part of her life that she loved and made her feel secure was to be taken away and there was nothing she could do to prevent it.

He was drunk again that night when she made the mistake of confronting him. 'You should have told me, Keith. I could have got a job years ago. We would have had a bit put by and...'

She saw the slap coming but couldn't avoid it. Putting her hand to her stinging cheek she ran from the room.

'What the hell could you do, woman? You're fucking useless.'

Marsha heard the words as she ran up the stairs and into their bedroom. She grabbed the door key from the top of her dressing table – she always kept it handy when he was out drinking – and locked the door. She sat on the floor with her knees to her chest and back against the door then listened. There was the usual crashing about and she wondered what he was breaking. They'd run out of ornaments long ago so perhaps it was the cheap crockery. There was silence after a few minutes but she gave it half an hour before getting up to use the bathroom. She usually checked on her husband but tonight Marsha didn't bother. *I hope the bastard dies in his sleep.* For the first time she realised it wasn't just an angry thought, but she actually meant it. After washing and taking her tablets Marsha returned to their room, locked the door and got into bed. Putting some cream on her cheek soothed it and it wasn't long before the pain- killers started to kick-in. There was nothing unusual about her night and she was soon sleeping soundly.

She arranged a house sale and sold as many of their belongings that they could manage without, giving them a little to live on while they showed people around. It was the usual mix of those genuinely interested and nosey people who had nothing better to do than look around others' homes.

7

They had a buyer! Her house was her pride and joy and it showed. Marsha was heartbroken and Keith was fuming. They'd accepted five thousand below the asking price at the bank's insistence. The mortgage and Keith's debt was paid off and they even had fifteen hundred pounds left.

'Transfer it to my account,' he told the bank clerk.

'No,' said Marsha. 'I want to open an account.'

It was the same clerk they'd dealt with about selling the house and she looked down at her desk, trying not to smile.

'You don't need an account, love. I'll handle this.'

Even though she recognised the warning in his voice, she stood her ground.

'I'm thirty next month, Keith and if I want a bank account, I'll open one,' she bit her bottom lip, realising she sounded like a five year old.

'I'll get the forms for you Mrs Lawson.' The bank clerk got up from her seat and turned to her filing cabinet.

'There's no need for that, love. My wife hasn't got any money to put into an account,' he laughed at the look Marsha gave him. 'Well you haven't.'

'Actually, Mr Lawson. Your wife has seven hundred and fifty pounds.'

He looked confused so she continued. 'Half of what's left after the mortgage and debt is paid off.'

'Now you listen here, love, that money...'

'That money, Mr Lawson belongs to you both. It was a joint mortgage was it not?'

'Yes but...'

'So legally half is yours and half is your wife's.'

'Fine.' It clearly wasn't fine and Marsha knew she'd get the brunt of his anger when they left.

She found out soon after that there was more than one way to skin a cat. He'd practically ignored her after the discussion in the bank, coming and going as he pleased without telling her what he was doing, though he did want her help in moving their few belongings from their home to his mother's garage. Ann showered sympathy on her son but practically ignored Marsha.

When they left his mother's Keith gave her the silent treatment once again. He'd never been able to look after himself so did talk to her if he wanted something to eat, drink, or to know where he'd put his keys, shirt or fags. They were now staying in emergency accommodation; a B&B provided by the local council, and were low down on the social housing list because they didn't have children. Marsha decided to look at the local rental market.

It was thoroughly depressing. Any half-decent place was way beyond what their benefits could afford and she didn't want to blow all of her savings in one go. There were some estates in the town with low-cost rental properties. Keith considered these to be *no go* areas and they were down to their last two days before being evicted from the B&B.

He disappeared again during their last day at the B&B. In desperation Marsha went to the library to use the free Internet. The friendly librarian helped her and it wasn't long before she was viewing properties in the area of Cornage, some thirty miles away. It would be a backward step but they could afford a shabby looking one-bedroom apartment, which would do until they were back on their feet. She hadn't told him yet but she planned to find a job so she could contribute to the household expenses. Returning to their temporary home in a hopeful mood, Marsha crossed her fingers that she could convince Keith to move location. At least he wouldn't use violence while they were in communal accommodation. One small step at a time, she wouldn't mention her plans to find a job yet.

He returned to the B&B looking smug.

'I have a new job.' He looked genuinely happy for the first time in ages.

'That's great, Keith. Tell me all about it.'

'I'll tell you on the way. Come on, let's get out of here.'

She put her own conversation on hold. She still intended to get herself a job but knew they'd have to go where his work took them for now.

'Where is it?' she called to his back as he walked down the path toward the rusty gate.

'Near Bloomington.'

Her heart sank and she knew what was coming next. 'We're going to live with my mother.'

'Oh no we're not. How can you expect...'

Keith dropped his bags and ran at his wife. She tensed. Even though he was quick tempered, he didn't usually show it outside their own four walls. He thrust his head forward into her face, invading her space.

'What I expect, woman, is for you to be grateful I've found a new job and my mother's agreed to put us up for a bit. Do you have any better ideas? Eh?'

'I was looking at properties in Cornage earlier,' she looked away, avoiding eye contact as she spoke. 'We could afford a small place there until we get back on our feet.'

'Cornage? Cornage? Are you totally stupid? There's no work there. How are we supposed to pay the bills and go out.'

'Well I don't go out. But I could get a job and...'

He laughed as if she'd said something hilariously funny.

'You. You get a job? Now you're really pushing it. What can you do Marsha and who the hell would employ you?'

'Well I...'

'Come on. We've got a bus to catch.'

He picked up his bags and she followed. Something had snapped and she was determined to show him and his unkind mother that she wasn't totally useless.

*****

Marsha had only been to Ann's house once, and that was before they were married. It looked shabbier from the outside than she recalled from years before and could do with a good scrub and a lick of paint. Keith had misplaced his key so rapped on the door. It opened slowly. Ann smiled at her son.

'Come in, son. And you.' She turned and walked back into the house. Keith followed his mother empty-handed and Marsha walked behind him with the bags she had carried from the bus stop. She went back outside to get her husband's bags. There wasn't much room as the hallway was filled with clutter, so she dropped the bags and stacked them on top of each other. There was a stale smell in the house as if the windows hadn't been opened for ages. She ignored it, not wanting to start off on the wrong foot with Ann, but was already starting to feel claustrophobic.

'Make a cuppa, Marsha then you can unpack while I sort things with my mother.'

She resisted the urge to curtsey and say *yes, M'lord.* These rebellious thoughts were coming more often and Marsha knew it was only a matter of time before they had a major bust-up. It was only the fear of him being violent that was keeping her quiet.

10

Ann was staring at the TV as if it were usual for her son and his wife to be moving in. The room was full of random bits and pieces, which Marsha tried her best to ignore.

'Is it okay to help myself to tea and coffee, Ann?'

'Tea, two sugars for me,' answered Ann without taking her eyes from the TV.

'Milk?'

'Of course. Don't ask stupid questions.'

The kitchen was like the rest of downstairs with every surface covered, some in paperwork, ornaments or bottles and packets on others. She took their tea into the room and Ann's only acknowledgement was, 'You're in the back room.'

'Upstairs on the right,' said Keith.

Marsha left them to it.

The stale air was worse upstairs and the smell hit her as soon as she opened the door. She had to squeeze between a bedside cabinet and lean over the boxes that were stacked, so she could reach to open the window. The bed was unmade and was covered in clothes and open packages containing bottles and tubes of face creams and all manner of toiletries. If they wanted to stay in this room most of the stuff would need to be moved. Ann had a three-bedroom house but Marsha couldn't move any of her belongings without talking to her first. Knowing her mother-in-law disliked her, she would need to speak to her husband. Keen to get everything sorted, she ran down the stairs.

'Have you got a minute, Keith? I need your help.'

He rolled his eyes at his mother. 'Can't you do anything, Marsha?'

Used to his snide comments she ignored him and made her way back upstairs. Keith followed.

'Oh for fuck's sake,' he said when he saw the state of the room. He went to the third room and Marsha followed. It wasn't much better. 'We need to move as much as we can into this one. Make a start and I'll have a word with mum.'

By the time Keith returned upstairs much later, Marsha had finished the work and there was now room for their belongings. A cobweb hung from the wardrobe to the ceiling and a dead fly lay in a layer of dust on the dressing table.

'I need to give it a clean before we can make ourselves at home in here, Keith. But I don't want to upset your mother.'

'She's fallen asleep watching the telly. Get some cleaning stuff from the kitchen and I'll go and get some fish and chips for our tea.'

By the time he returned stinking of drink more than three hours later, their room looked clean and homely, with their own bedding and a fresh smell.

It took a few weeks for Keith's temporary clearance to be issued for his new job at Bloomington Barracks. He'd been moping around the house and drinking too much when he went out. Marsha recognised the signs but he could either hide them from his mother or she chose to ignore them. She sighed with relief the day he left the house to start work. The barracks was out in the sticks; an eight-mile bus ride from his mother's house and one mile walk from the nearest stop. The last mile wasn't on the route so Keith walked for the first few days until he discovered that a bus for workers at the barracks stopped there. He didn't use this for long as he'd arranged a lift with one of his new work mates who lived nearby. He settled in quickly and started to enjoy his new job.

Marsha felt like an unpaid slave. They didn't even have a settling in period where Ann pretended to like her company. She seemed over the moon that the prodigal son had returned but it was hard to tell. She was pretty much indifferent to everything and spent her time in front of the television. Even then she seemed to be in a world of her own. Despite her indifference, she made it clear that Marsha was an unwanted guest at best.

'Keep out of my way and make yourself useful.' They were the most words she'd said so far. Ann didn't do anything but despite the occasional horrible comment directed towards her, Marsha felt sorry for the woman. Something wasn't quite right.

Marsha enjoyed cleaning so spent her days doing housework. It took ages, as Ann wasn't prepared to throw out any of her items, even though most of them looked like junk to her daughter-in-law. Within a few weeks the whole place had been deep cleaned and looked better than it ever had. She had been careful not to comment on the amount of clutter but despite this, the cleaning and cooking, Ann was still cold and distant. She would snipe at Marsha at every opportunity and it took a will of iron for her daughter-in-law to keep quiet. After almost three weeks she'd run out of sympathy and Marsha could take no more.

'Your house was dirty and unwelcoming, Ann. I've made it sparkle and it looks like a proper home now, and all you can do is criticise.' She was as surprised at her own words as both her husband and mother-in-law were. After a few moments silence Ann found her voice.

'Are you going to let her speak to me like that, Keith?'

'That was out of order, Marsha. Apologise now.'

Did he think she was a child? She looked at them in turn. They both honestly expected her to say sorry. In the past she would have mumbled an apology simply to keep the peace, but something had changed. The worse they could do was throw her out and she wasn't frightened any more. She had nowhere to go but even living on the streets had to be better than this.

'I won't apologise for being honest,' she folded her arms. 'I am happy to clean and cook in exchange for bed and board, but I will not be treated like an unpaid slave. If you want me to leave I'll go and pack my things now and...'

'Don't be stupid, Marsha. You're my wife. You're not going anywhere!'

'Don't call me stupid, Keith.'

'What the?...'

'Perhaps she's got a point son, she is a hard worker...'

'I am here you know.' *Marsha wondered if she'd entered a parallel universe where her mother-in-law actually gave a damn.*

'So you're taking her side now, even though I stuck up for you? I'll never understand bloody women as long as I live.'

Ann actually smirked and Marsha looked down trying not to laugh. It was a turning point. She was thirty years old but felt like a naughty schoolgirl. Something had changed and she regretted not speaking out earlier. Unable to look her husband in the eye she didn't want to wind him up.

'I'll make a cup of tea.'

Marsha headed for the kitchen. For once, her mother-in-law didn't slag her off as soon as she was out of sight.

A cease-fire ensued during the next few days but Marsha noticed a change in the atmosphere. Keith went out after his dinner every night so she decided to try harder with Ann, in the hope she'd come out of herself. She was pleasant to her but all she initially got for her troubles were monosyllabic responses to any comments or questions, or stiff polite answers. When alone with

13

her thoughts, Marsha wondered if she was the problem. Her alcoholic mother had hated her and now her mother-in-law appeared to despise her, despite her best efforts.

Keith announced he was going out after finishing his tea on Thursday evening. 'I'm taking Marsha with me, Mum. Give you a bit of peace.'

'Fine,' said Ann as she left the table and picked up her knitting.

'Go on then, love. Get the dishes done then go and get yourself ready.' He smacked her backside as Marsha got up to take the plates to the kitchen.

This was a new turn of events. She hadn't been out for a drink with him in ages and she was quite excited. Marsha rushed through her chores and ran upstairs to get ready.

'You've brushed up well.' Keith said as she entered the living room. He was being uncharacteristically considerate and she didn't show her surprise, for fear of annoying him. They said goodbye to his mother.

He walked in front of her towards the bus stop, but stopped suddenly and turned. 'I don't know what's come over you but if you're ever rude to my mother again, girl, I'll make sure you eat your words. Understand?'

'But that's all blown over, Keith. We're fine now and getting on well.'

He ignored her comment. Grabbing her arm he squeezed it tight.

'Ouch.'

An old couple tutted as they passed so Keith loosened his grip. 'Understand?' It came out as a growl and Marsha was left in no doubt as to his intentions. She'd expected him to have a go earlier in the week so this came as a surprise. It was a front and he hadn't changed at all.

'Now we're going to meet some of the people I work with so cheer up. I don't want them thinking I'm married to a miserable cow.'

Although disappointed at her husband's words, Marsha was still glad to be going out and excited at the prospect of meeting new people. They didn't speak on the bus and she looked out of the window as the houses became sparse and the countryside took over. They were heading out to the sticks to a new area as well as new people. Getting off the bus he told her

14

they were going to *The Black Horse.* The pub was at the end of a lane, a few miles from the base and she imagined, the local for those living on the camp. It was great to be out of the house and she might actually have a conversation with someone other than her husband, mother-in-law or the checkout staff where she did their weekly shop.

She followed Keith to the bar and as he ordered a pint for himself and a glass of wine for her, somebody called to him.

'Yo, Keith. Over here.'

'Be there in a minute, Sam.' He paid for the drinks and made his way to his friends. Marsha followed, trying to take everything in as she did so. The interior looked comfortable with a number of booths against the walls and tables in the centre of the room. Some of the tables were occupied by fit looking young men and one of them winked at her cheekily when Keith had his back to him. Marsha blushed and looked away.

The man called Sam and some others had pulled two tables together. 'Sit here, love, next to Carol.' He introduced himself and everybody else. 'Don't worry, I won't be testing you later.' They all laughed and Marsha immediately warmed to the man.

Carol explained that Sam was her husband. He was the charge hand for the drivers and she also worked on the base, in one of the offices. She said that she worked for the company that employed cleaners, cooks, receptionists, clerical staff and a number of other people.

Keith was totally engrossed in a football conversation so Marsha didn't think he'd hear their discussion. 'Oh I would love to have a job,' she confided in Carol. 'Keith wasn't keen for me to work while he was at the Steel Works but now I'm desperate to get something.'

'You live with your mother-in-law don't you?'

'Hmm,' said Marsha.

'Yeah I'd be desperate to get out of the house too if I lived with mine.' They both laughed and Marsha was surprised at how deep Carol's laugh was.

'What are you two laughing about?' asked Sam.

Carol noticed the warning look Keith gave his wife and Marsha trying to avoid eye contact.

'Period pains and other girls talk,' she said. 'That did the trick,' she whispered to Marsha as the men quickly turned away

15

and returned to their football talk. 'What sort of job are you looking for?'

'It would only be cleaning. I can't do anything else.'

'They always need new staff on the base. Shall I have a look for you and get you an application form if they need anyone?'

'You'd do that?'

'Yes of course. Give me your mobile number and we can arrange to meet up.'

Marsha took her phone out of her pocket. Seeing Carol's face she gave an apologetic look.

'Oh my God, Marsha. That's a proper brick. We need to bring you into the twenty first century.' They laughed again and the men shook their heads this time.

They exchanged numbers and Marsha also gave her mother-in-law's landline. 'In case this runs out of credit.'

'How about we meet for a coffee on Saturday and I can let you know then?'

'That would be great.'

'Okay. Ten o'clock at Costas in town? I'll find out what's available and we can have a proper chat.'

Marsha agreed, at the same time wondering what to tell Keith and his mother. She knew her way around town from doing the grocery shopping and had seen people enjoying each other's company in the coffee shop. Now she was going to be one of those people.

'Thanks, Carol. I appreciate your help.'

'No bother.' Carol felt sorry for the woman and was determined to get her a job. Although she wasn't involved with recruiting, Rose from the netball club might be able to pull some strings. The players helped each other out if they could so Carol was confident she could get Marsha to the interview stage at least. It wasn't difficult to get a cleaning job on the base as people were always looking to climb the ladder, which created lots of vacancies.

*****

Keith had arranged to play football on Saturday morning. He handed her twenty quid.

'Go and do a bit of shopping and make the three of us something special for tea tonight,' he winked and smacked her behind. 'You know what I like.'

16

Marsha was walking on air.

'So what delights can we expect this evening?' asked Ann after Keith left the house.

'I was going to cook a curry.' She knew her mother-in-law hated hot food.

'But,' Ann tutted. 'You know I don't like…'

'Only kidding, Ann. I thought I'd do steak in pepper sauce with peas and chips and a trifle for afters. What do you think?'

'That's hardly what I'd call special.'

She sounded like a spoilt kid but it washed over Marsha who was determined not to let her mother-in-law spoil her good mood.

'I can cook you something different if you like? What do you fancy?'

'Liver and onions is my favourite.' Ann was surprised but answered quickly, hoping Marsha meant it.

'Okay, no problemo.' She hated liver but would make the effort if it would keep the peace.

Ann didn't know what had come over her daughter-in-law but was happy to take advantage of her good mood. She reached for her purse. 'Here,' she handed her a fiver. 'Get a bottle of sparkling wine from Aldi and we'll make a night of it.'

'Thank you, Ann. That's kind,' she meant it and Ann looked genuinely happy at the compliment.

Marsha reflected on their conversation while on the bus on the way to town. So they could both be civil to each other but it required immense effort, for Marsha anyway. Could this be a new chapter in her life? No nastiness from her mother-in-law, the chance she may get a job and the possibility of a new friend in Carol? She certainly hoped so.

Chapter 3

Penny checked into the hotel and signed the registration in her maiden name. She noticed the receptionist had simply added *plus one* next to her name on the form. Good man.

'Your usual suite Ms Forbes?' he asked.

'Yes please,' she smiled and took the key card for room 257.

Gordon the receptionist watched her walk towards the lift. She'd been staying at *The Royal* on a regular basis for almost two years and was a good customer. Although always courteous, she couldn't be bothered to look at his badge or make an effort to use his first name. She always booked the same suite at the end corner of the second floor. It had a panoramic view of the town but more importantly, assumed Gordon, guests wouldn't wander down that corridor because it only led to room 257. Gordon's boyfriend worked in the Spa so he knew Penny's routine well enough. First she'd use the gymnasium then cool off in the pool. She'd return to her suite and shortly after, if he wasn't busy, he'd see her latest enter the hotel and go straight to the lift. He wondered if it would still be the Syrian; this one had lasted longer than the others, about six months so far if Gordon's memory served him correctly. After a few hours they'd order room service. Sometimes the Syrian would stay overnight, others he'd leave and she would spend the night on her own. The following morning she usually had a massage followed by breakfast, before checking out. Ms Forbes was a creature of habit.

Penny lay in bed checking out her Facebook feed while waiting for Sayid. Three taps on the door signalled his arrival. She stood up slowly, slipped out of her bra and knickers and donned her full-length sheer negligee. She opened the door, popped her head around it to ensure it was Sayid, then beckoned him in.

Her negligee left nothing to the imagination and he couldn't help himself. He embraced her and his mouth engulfed hers in a passionate kiss. When he broke for air he surveyed the vision in front of him and knew he was blessed. Penelope hadn't told him her age. He knew she was older but she was in fantastic shape and she'd chosen him. Out of all the men she could have picked, he'd struck lucky. He reached for her again but she laughed and held back.

'Go and change first. He's away for another month.' So today she wanted it rough. He grabbed his bag and headed for the bathroom. Now used to Penelope's fantasies, he didn't mind at all and took his time to get the details right; it was important to her.

Penny lay on her side on the bed and squeezed her nipples in turn until they stood to attention under her negligee. She smiled as she watched Sayid walk to the bed from the bathroom. The black linen tunic covered him from neck to knee and was suitably adorned with heavy gold necklaces. The Egyptian headdress suited him perfectly as she knew it would and the gold belt and sash hanging from his waist, together with the leather sandals, completed the look. He was her Pharaoh and Penny felt herself growing hot at the sight. The muscles in his toned arms bulged and she was eager to run her hands over his body.

'Do as you will, my Pharaoh.'

'On your front!'

She wasn't quick enough to turn around so Sayid took hold of her and turned her onto her front. He was a bit rough but Penny enjoyed it. He lifted her body so she was kneeling on all fours. Sayid ripped off the negligee, straddled his slave and, without warning, thrust his hard penis into her. She lifted her head and cried out as he grabbed her breasts and fondled them before pinching her nipples. He could feel her excitement and his next move took every bit of willpower he possessed. Without warning, he withdrew.

'No, Sayid. Pleeeeeaaaase.'

He turned her onto her back and pushed against her teasingly. 'What do you want, Penelope?'

'I want you, my Pharaoh. I beg of you.' She lifted her body towards him. He ignored her, instead he dangled his cock over her face and Penny took the hint. She saw the intense pleasure on his face as she sucked him off, her hands working on his balls in rhythm with her mouth. He could hold it no longer and Penny turned to the side as he emptied his seed onto the sheets. After a few deep breaths he spoke.

'Did you think we'd finished, slave?' He ripped off his costume and picked up the Kurbash with his right hand, tapping his left palm menacingly.

19

It was her turn and she prepared for the onslaught, glad that Paul wasn't home for a while. The pain was sickly sweet and she cried out in ecstasy when she could take no more.

Much later, Penny watched as Sayid headed for the bathroom. Now naked, she felt an urge to jump out of bed and squeeze his tight butt. As she turned she knew that making love again would be extremely painful. The next time would have to be safe and gentle. She didn't mind, she looked at the Kurbash on the floor. With its gold handle and black leather strips the whip matched his outfit and was certainly fit for a Pharaoh. She imagined the masters using the very same on their subjects and slaves in ancient Egypt. Penny knew she would have been the one who used the Kurbash had she lived in those days, and not the one on the receiving end. Despite the pain she couldn't feel any tears on her skin so Sayid had been careful as well as masterful. She would still bruise but the bruises would be gone by Paul's return and he wouldn't suspect anything. As for the other pain, it was a small price to pay for such pleasure and a little Vaseline would do the trick.

She thought about her other lovers. The Syrian had lasted the longest but Penny knew it could complicate matters if she kept the arrangement going for too long. He seemed a bit too keen and it was a worry. She'd meant to end it today but after his performance, decided to keep him for a while longer. Now that Kaitlyn was at university she needed something more than just a quick wham bang when Paul was away. Sayid was a pleasant way of passing the time when she didn't have a match, training, lunch or shopping dates with one of the other wives. She thought about their daughter. She'd always been her father's little girl and they weren't particularly close. When Kaitlyn was growing up Penny had found it difficult having to manage the home, find the time to take her daughter to school or her after-school clubs, and to play netball. Now she had her life back, she intended to make the most of it.

'Champagne, Penelope?' She must have nodded off so opened her eyes at the sound of his voice. He was standing naked at her side of the bed and although still sore, her body ached for him. She'd never experienced sex like this before.

'Come here, my sexy Syrian, but be gentle.'

'Yes, my lady,' he put the champagne bottle down and hovered over her, leaning in with a gentle kiss. She sucked his lips

20

and he felt his passion reach his groin. Penny groaned, ready to be consumed by pleasure.

She would have been surprised to discover her daughter was also in a hotel room in another town, but similar situation.

*****

Kaitlyn watched with more curiosity than satisfaction as Martin grunted then collapsed onto her. She pushed him, ensuring she wasn't too rough, then he smiled and took the hint. Rolling off her he kissed her forehead. Within seconds he was snoring gently.

She watched dispassionately as his chest moved up and down. She'd promised herself she would only go with fit men but the money had been far too tempting. It beat working her butt off in a pub and though it wasn't particularly pleasant work, it gave her the lifestyle she deserved and kept her parents off her back. Her friend Evie had been amazed when she took her home for a week the previous summer. Most of her uni friends thought her family was as broke and average as theirs and Evie thought it was a wind-up as Kaitlyn drove her mini up the drive to the mansion.

'Who the hell lives here, Kat?'

'I do.'

'Yeah right, and a pig's arse ain't pork.'

'Seriously, I do. My father's a self-made millionaire. He has a chain of pawnbrokers and is in the recycling business.'

'So he got all this,' she swept her hand around in a circle, 'through other people's crap.'

Kaitlyn laughed. 'Yeah, that's about right. But don't put it like that to him.'

'No, of course I won't.'

'So why do you need to...' Evie had the same job as Kaitlyn. It was a secret that only the two knew about, except for the agency and the men who bought their services.

'While my parents are happy to fund my studies so I leave uni without any debts, my father is unwilling to fund what he calls my *high maintenance* lifestyle. He says hard work can only make you a better person so insisted I get a part-time job.'

'So he thinks...'

'Yup. Both my parents think I work in a bar but you know how much that pays.'

'But what about your mother, doesn't she give you anything without your father knowing?'

21

Kaitlyn sighed. 'My mother doesn't work and *barely has enough to fund her own necessities* as she puts it. Like going away for weekends, lunching with other rich bitches and buying designer everything.'

'I see.' Evie didn't want to mention it but Kat seemed to have many of her mother's traits. 'Who are you like?'

'Well I'm sporty like my mother and determined like my father but that's about it. Let's go and meet them then you can tell me what you think. Oh and don't tell anyone else about my background. Uni is the only place where people see me for myself, and not Paul and Penny Mason's daughter.'

'Of course, you know you can trust me. But what if they find out about how you really earn your money?'

'How could that possibly happen?'

It was a fair point.

Chapter 4

Marsha had enjoyed a coffee and a laugh with Carol. They hit it off and she already knew she'd found a good friend.

'Do you want to take this away to complete and give it to Keith to give to me?' She handed Marsha the application form for a cleaning position.

'No, I umm...'

'So you haven't told him yet?'

'How did you know?'

'It was pretty obvious,' she laughed. 'It's not a problem but you're going to have to tell him some time.'

'I know. I'm cooking us all a special tea tonight. Hopefully he'll be in a good mood if they won the match today.'

'And if he isn't?'

'I'm going to get a job whether it's this one or something else, so Keith and his mother will just have to deal with it. Actually, she was really nice to me this morning, so I thought the real Ann must have been kidnapped.' They laughed together easily. Carol's laugh was so deep and loud that other customers stared and some laughed with them.

'Fill in the form then and I'll get us both another coffee.' Carol stood up but sat down again when she saw Marsha's expression. 'What is it?'

'I'm not very good at this sort of thing, I'm dyslexic so...well, you know.'

'Okay. Carol passed her a pen.'

'You're not going to help me. I thought...'

'Help, yes. Do it for you? No.'

Fair enough thought Marsha as Carol guided her through the application. 'What's this one about vetting?'

'Oh yeah. Because we're on a military base you have to be checked out so they can see you're not a terrorist or a spy.'

'As if. What happens if I don't want to give out details about my family?'

'If they can't check your background, Marsha, they won't give you a job. Is there a problem?'

She could see Marsha withdrawing into herself. 'They treat all this information on a *need to know* basis and keep it private after they've done whatever checks they have to do. It's

23

all in line with one act or another and they're pretty serious about data protection.'

Marsha didn't have a clue what she was talking about but knew if she wanted the job she'd have to take the plunge. She wasn't ready to tell Carol about her past so if her new friend wanted to look at the form when they went their separate ways later, that was entirely up to her.

'We've all got a past, Marsha. People understand that.'

She ignored her and they moved on to the next questions.

When the form was completed Carol sealed it in an envelope. 'I'll give this to Sandy on Monday. I'll phone your mobile or the landline to let you know the next stage.'

Marsha nodded. 'I'm going to buy a decent mobile phone with my first pay packet.'

'Or you could ask Keith to get you one now?' she changed the subject. 'Do you fancy doing a bit of shopping?' Carol could have kicked herself when she saw the look on Marsha's face. 'I meant window-shopping. I'm a bit skint until the end of the month.'

Marsha relaxed. 'Yeah, me too. Well I'm skint most of the time to be honest, that's why I really need this job.'

Heading out of the door, they crossed the road and made their way to the Mall. It was like being a teenager again before all her problems started and the time flew by. She looked at her watch and was surprised to see it was one o'clock. 'Oh Christ. I'm sorry, Carol but I have to go. I need to do the shopping then get home to cook the dinner.'

'Okay, Cinders. I'll phone as soon as Sandy gets back to me about this,' she waved the envelope. 'We must do this again soon, it's been fun.'

Carol reached over and they kissed on both cheeks then said their goodbyes. Marsha did her shopping and was still on a high as she got off the bus and made her way to Ann's house.

Keith was already home. 'You took your time.'

'I met up with Carol and we went window-shopping. I've applied for a cleaning job on the base, Keith.' She held her breath. There it was out in the open.

'What do you mean you've applied for a job? No wife of mine...'

'Perhaps it's for the best, Keith,' his mother interrupted. 'If you're not going to have a family, Marsha should go out to work. Bring in some money instead of being stuck in the house all day.'

'Thank you, Ann.' Marsha meant it.

'Keep out of this, Mum, and who said we're not going to have a family?'

'Well I'm sorry. But I just assumed...' she looked from one to the other. 'You've been married for ages and if you haven't had children yet, you either don't want them or there's a problem.'

So her real mother-in-law had indeed been kidnapped and replaced with this one who was caring and sensitive, but still extremely nosey.

'It's Marsha, Mum. She can't...'

How bloody dare he! Marsha saw red. 'It's not me at all as well you know. There's nothing wrong with me, Ann.'

'I don't understand, Marsha. Have you had tests? Keith didn't mention?'

Keith ignored his mother's confusion. How dare his wife imply he was something less than a man. 'Come with me, Marsha, now. I'll show you that everything's in perfect working order.' He grabbed for her hand but she dodged him.

'I think I'll pass, Keith.'

'Come with me now!'

She ran around to the back of the settee where he couldn't reach her. 'Get off, Keith. You can't make me.'

'I can and I will. He lunged towards her.' His mother had seen enough.

'Stop it, Keith. Now!' He halted in his tracks.

'You can't force yourself on her, Son, even if she is your wife.'

All the fight went out of him and he slumped onto the settee. Now even his mother was on his wife's side, he'd soon put paid to that. Keith gave Marsha a sly look but she didn't see what was coming.

'She had a kid when she was fourteen, Mum, and her alcoholic mother made her give it up for adoption.'

Ann could see by Marsha's face that her son was telling the truth. 'So you've been married for all this time and didn't think to tell me about this?'

'It's not that simple, Ann. My mother...'

'I was talking to my son, not his slut of a wife.'

So the judgemental Ann was back, but she'd got it all wrong. 'I'm not a slut, Ann, it wasn't like that...'

'Shut up and get out of my sight.'

Marsha went to their room because she didn't have anywhere else to go. Her alcoholic mother had died four years before, her daughter was with her adopted family wherever that may be, and the man who had raped her? He was one of her mother's short-term boyfriends. She hoped he was rotting in hell somewhere. She curled up on the bed and cried. The sooner she got a job and could take some control of her life, the better.

Marsha occupied herself with household chores over the coming days. To her surprise, her mother-in-law's attitude softened towards her, despite the news about the baby and calling her a slut. She couldn't work her out but was relieved all the same. Ann was making a real effort. She seemed to enjoy Marsha's company and was taking an interest in the kitchen. She hadn't learnt to cook properly so wasn't confident and explained that before they came to live with her, she ate the same food day in day out. Marsha was a good teacher and Ann relished her new role as chef's assistant. She couldn't stand housework but was happy to try out new recipes under supervision. Marsha would write a note or give instructions and get on with other household chores while Ann experimented. It seemed to work well and lightened her load. As life with her mother-in-law improved, it deteriorated with her husband. Keith's way of punishing her was to go out every night. Feeling braver with her mother-in-law present, she tried to talk to him about booking tests for them both so they could start a family, but he refused point blank. It drove a wedge between them and his way of dealing with it was to criticise his wife.

'You probably damaged yourself by having a kid so young. You'd be a rubbish mother anyway.' Ann had taken Marsha's side when Keith made that cruel remark.

'That's right. You take her side. Typical bloody women sticking together.'

'I'm on the side of fairness, Keith. That's all.'

'And I'm off out.' He'd slammed the door behind him and both women were happy he was out of the house, but neither voiced her opinion.

*****

It was two weeks before Marsha heard from Carol. She thought she'd gone off her and put it down to experience. She was upstairs vacuuming when Ann shouted.

'Marsha. There's a Carol on the phone for you, love.'

She stumbled down the last three stairs but managed to stop herself from crashing into the wall in her haste to get to the phone. 'Hi, Carol. Good to hear from you.'

'Hi, Marsha. You sound breathless. Are you okay?'

'Yeah, just rushing about as usual. But never mind me, you sound rough.'

Carol explained she'd been off work with a worse than usual bout of flu. 'I'm so sorry, that's why I haven't been in touch. I'm on the mend now though and returned to the office today. Sandy was all over me like a bad rash. They're short staffed and desperate to recruit. I have a letter here for you offering you an interview this Friday.'

'This Friday?'

Carol could hear the panic in her voice. Fair enough for a thirty year old who hadn't yet worked.

'You'll be fine, Marsha. We could meet up beforehand if you like and I'll go through some of the questions with you.'

'That'd be great. When's good for you?'

They arranged to meet at Costa Coffee the following evening after Carol finished work. Although she felt more confident about the interview, Marsha was still terrified come the Friday morning. Dressed in her black skirt and white blouse wearing sensible shoes and her knee-length old coat, she waited for the bus. This time she didn't notice the views of the countryside as she mentally rehearsed the possible questions and her answers. She walked from the bus stop to the main gate and told the guard she was there for an interview. She was then invited into the security box until a cheerful sounding girl with a foreign accent made an appearance.

'Hi, you must be Marsha?'

Marsha stood up and nodded. 'I'm Sandy.' She was almost six foot and well built, with the biggest smile that Marsha had ever seen. She guessed she was the Fijian woman who played netball with Carol.

'I'll take you to the office where Rose and Sasha are going to interview you. Don't look so worried. You'll be fine. I play netball with both of them and they're very nice people, even though Rose is a bit bossy. Sasha's very fit and doesn't know how to keep still. Do you live around here? More importantly do you play netball? We have a club here where we all meet on Wednesday evenings and we play in the league on Tuesdays and Thursdays. We have two tournaments in the winter and we also have a summer league. Oh, and we have a tournament in the spring too. Are you interested?'

She talked non-stop until they reached the building. It took Marsha's mind off the interview and she forgot how nervous she was until they arrived. The building they entered looked like an old-fashioned hut that Marsha would expect to see in an old black and white war movie.

'Our offices are being renovated,' Sandy explained. 'We're here on a temporary basis until we can move back in. Take a seat there and I'll tell them you've arrived.'

Within a few minutes Sandy returned with a slim woman who was wearing a uniform. She introduced herself as Sasha. 'I'm interviewing you today with Rose, our boss. Please don't worry. Carol speaks highly of you so just be yourself and answer the questions as honestly as you can. This way.'

Sandy mouthed *good luck* and closed the door behind them.

There was one other woman in the office. Dressed in what Marsha would describe as posh office clothing, she looked very business-like and not particularly friendly. She didn't look up and as Sasha sat next to her, Marsha wasn't sure what she should do. Perhaps she hadn't heard them come in. She was about to say something when the woman put down her pen and leaned over the desk to shake Marsha's hand.

'Hello, I'm Rose and I'm in charge around here.'

They shook hands. 'Pleased to meet you. I'm Marsha.'

'Yes I gathered that. Take a seat.'

The woman terrified her so Marsha sat down and waited.

'Tell me about yourself.' She didn't look up as Marsha explained that she had enjoyed keeping her own home in immaculate condition until they sold it, and now she was happy to cook and clean for her mother-in-law. All the while Sasha was fiddling with papers or picking up a pen or pencil then putting it down. Marsha tried not to get distracted.

'What about previous jobs? Sasha didn't give me a CV.'

'That's because I don't have one. My husband asked me to be a stay at home wife and before that I spent four years caring for my mother on a daily basis before she died, so...' She didn't know what else to say.

'Okay. Tell me what are your strengths?'

'I'm a hard worker and easy going so get on with most people.' Rose looked satisfied with her answer so Marsha made a mental note to thank Carol.

'Any weaknesses?' asked Rose.

'Chocolate.'

Sasha had taken a drink of water and spurted half of it over the table as she burst out laughing. Rose almost smiled.

'And lack of experience in the workplace but I'm quick to learn and I know how to clean so I don't think that will be a problem.'

'Quite.' Rose scribbled some more notes. 'Over to you, Sasha.'

Sasha took a moment to compose herself before speaking. 'I'm going to ask you some general questions about cleaning now, Marsha, to find out whether we think you're suitable for the post. Let's start with what products you would use to clean a toilet?'

Now on a subject she knew lots about, Marsha answered Sasha's questions with ease and soon forgot her nervousness. Both Rose and Sasha knew they'd offer her the job but Rose didn't give out good news so easily.

'That's everything from us, Marsha. Do you have any questions?'

Carol had told her to ask a few questions so she fired away.

'When will I know if I've been successful?'

'Very soon,' said Rose. 'Anything else?'

She forgot what she was going to say so shook her head.

'Thank you. Please take a seat outside and we'll call you back in once we've made our decision.'

Marsha said thanks and headed for the door.

'Yes, Sasha?' asked Rose.

'Of course. She seems keener than most. I think she'll be good.'

'Okay.' Rose finished her paperwork before looking at Sasha. 'Did you phone Penny to ask if Kaitlyn can play next Tuesday? The Eagles are our hardest opposition this season.'

'I'm not sure about that, Rose, I thought the...'

'Trust me. Now they've got a new coach and their Goal Attack is awesome. I might play Keeper then we can put Kaitlyn at Goal Defence. She'll need to come to training next Wednesday though so we can see if it works and so there's not any bitching about her being selected when she hasn't been. You know what some of them are like.'

'I spoke to Penny who said Kaitlyn won't be able to play. She's not due home from uni yet.'

'Shit, must have got the dates wrong again. I wish some of the players would learn to prioritise their lives, I'll need to come up with a Plan B later.'

Kaitlyn's education was more important that their netball match but Sasha resisted the urge to tell Rose. She clicked the top of her pen repeatedly.

'Put the bloody pen down!' Sasha did as bid and tried to keep her hands still.

'Shall we get Marsha back in to give her the good news?'

Sasha was glad of an excuse to move. She nodded, then left the room to call Marsha back in.

*****

She was walking on air when she shared her good news with her mother-in-law. Marsha had made a delicious stew for her and Keith, and Ann had cooked herself liver and onions. The women hoped that Keith would be pleasant but their optimism was short-lived and so was Marsha's good mood.

'So, despite what I want, you've decided you're going to work anyway? And at the base where I work?'

'Look, Keith. It won't hurt us. In fact we'll be better off and we can start to save and maybe look for a new...'

'You've gone against my wishes and I don't want to discuss it.'

So that was that. They ate the meal in silence and Keith left the house as soon as he'd finished.

'I don't know if I can take much more of this.' Marsha knew it wasn't a good idea to whinge to Ann, but the words had slipped out.

'Come on, love. I'll help you with the dishes. Then I thought we could go out for a game of bingo.'

'What?'

She was used to Ann helping occasionally but they never went out.

'I used to play years ago. I went to the club earlier and got us both free membership, so we only pay for the games. It's my treat tonight. What do you think?'

So her husband was a bastard but her mother-in-law was turning into a friend. Life wasn't so bad after all.

'I'm up for it.'

Chapter 5

Over three weeks passed before Marsha got the call confirming her start date. It was Sandy.

'Your temporary clearance has come through to work on the base. Can you come in next Monday to do all the paperwork?'

'Yes, what time?'

'Eight-thirty. We'll also issue you with your uniform so you can start as soon as everything is signed.'

'That's great, Sandy.'

'I'll meet you at the gate again. See you then.'

She said thanks and goodbye. As soon as she hung up, the phone rang again. This time it was Carol asking if she was free to meet for coffee and a natter the following Saturday. With Keith doing his own thing during the evenings and at weekends, Marsha agreed without hesitation. She was a lot happier since starting to go out with Ann on Fridays and meeting up with Carol occasionally. And now she had a job to look forward to. She put her problems with Keith on the back burner, hoping he would accept their new life. Deep down she wasn't optimistic but life was going well for her and her husband's attitude upset her less than she thought it would.

Their hours were different, so Marsha didn't travel into work with Keith. Day three into her new job and she was enjoying it. It was only cleaning and some looked down their noses at the cleaners but that didn't bother her. She was doing what she would have been doing at home and being paid for her efforts, so life was good. She was also getting used to the banter with the other women, until one of them decided to spoil it.

Marsha was told to report to the empty office block that had recently been renovated. She was to start at one end and her unknown colleague at the other. They were meant to meet in the middle. As she worked she listened to a song and wondered where the radio was. When the singer coughed, Marsha realised it was the other cleaner. The woman had a lovely voice and from the song choices, was a country music fan. It was good having music while she cleaned and she soon worked her way through the offices, getting closer to the voice as she did so. She was a little taken aback as she entered the last office in the block, the one where the singing was coming from. The woman was surrounded by cleaning kit, but it looked as if very little had been used. She was looking out of the window and coming to the end of *Nine to Five*.

'Hi, I'm Marsha, the new cleaner,' she smiled nervously.

'So you are,' said the singer. 'I'm going for a cigarette.' She didn't return her smile and bumped into Marsha on the way out of the door, despite there being plenty of space to avoid her. They were supposed to be sharing the cleaning; Marsha had worked her way through the block cleaning all offices on her own except the one she was standing in. The singer hadn't lifted a finger and her attitude towards Marsha sucked. Having not met her before, Marsha's good mood disappeared and she wondered how she could have possibly upset the woman. She also wondered how someone with such a sweet voice could be so nasty. Perhaps it was because she was new and the singing woman would mellow.

She didn't.

Her nemesis, Suzanne, was probably in her late teens or early twenties and reminded Marsha of the bullies who'd picked on her before she left school. She was also a lazy cow and spent more time avoiding work than it would take to do the job. She bitched about people but it riled her when Marsha refused to join in.

On the Friday morning one of the older women pulled Marsha to one side. 'You're cramping our style, love, you need to put the brakes on.'

'Eh?' Marsha didn't have a clue what she was talking about.

'Look. We know you're new and keen and all that, but you make the rest of us look as if we're not pulling our weight. You don't need to go so fast.'

'But I'm not. C'mon, Lil. It's not like I'm breaking any records here. We're only cleaning offices for God's sake.'

Lil stirred her tea. 'I can tell you now Suzanne isn't very happy. Your name is shit and you've only started this week. You don't want to make an enemy of her, love.'

'I'm only doing my job!'

'Think about it, love,' she picked up her mug. 'I'm going for a fag.'

Marsha sighed. She didn't need this aggravation when her life was starting to get better. Perhaps she'd go straight home from work tonight instead of giving the netball training a go. She knew Carol would feel let down and didn't want to disappoint her new friend, especially since she'd played a big part in getting her this job. She reluctantly changed into her new sports kit - thank God for Lidl - and met Carol after work as arranged.

'Don't look so nervous, you'll love it.'

She resisted the urge to say *whatever* and changed the subject. 'Do you know Suzanne?'

'The stroppy cow with a beautiful voice who thinks the world owes her a living?'

'That sounds about right. She doesn't like me.'

Carol knew Marsha was pretty nervous about playing netball, so decided not to tell her that Suzanne would be there. She was a different woman on the netball court and she came alive when she played. As long as they didn't socialise with her or listen to any of her bitchiness, they'd do okay.

'I shouldn't worry, she doesn't like anyone unless they've got meat and two veg?' said Carol.

Marsha laughed but blushed at her friend's explanation.

'You have led a sheltered life haven't you?'

'So she's a slapper?' asked Marsha.

'Yup. But you meet her sister Chardonnay and they're like chalk and cheese.'

'Who would call their kid Chardonnay?'

'That's netball. You meet all kinds of interesting people.'

Marsha decided to wait and see.

*****

Carol had already explained the rules so they spent a little time going through the basic passes for Marsha to get a feel for the ball, and for the others to observe her abilities. Carol was pleasantly surprised at her hand to eye coordination and spatial awareness. By the look on Sandy's face, she was also impressed. They made her run and jump for the ball and although a little awkward trying to remember the footwork rules, she was a quick learner.

'I can't believe she hasn't played since school,' said Sandy. 'She's got bags of potential.'

'I agree,' said Carol. 'She's going to be a star, not only at netball.' Sandy wanted to know what she meant but Marsha ran to them with the ball, panting but looking full of life.

'Right then, what's next?'

'The basics of defending. What do you reckon, Sandy?'

34

'Let's do it. Marsha, you feed the ball to Carol then watch what I do. I'll explain as we go along.'

When it was Marsha's turn to mark Carol with Sandy feeding the ball, she was all over the place to start with. Carol dodged and feinted moves and Marsha didn't have a clue where she was or where she was going.

'Hang on,' said Sandy. 'Stand sideways on to Carol and when she moves, you move.' She demonstrated, then threw the ball and watched as Marsha jumped, the tips of her fingers just missing the ball.

'That's better. Remember what we said. One eye on your player and the other on the ball.'

She missed the first few passes and still looked around doing a good meerkat impression when trying to follow or keep up with Carol. Before they took a break some of the information was beginning to stick and Carol had to work a lot harder to get free for the ball. When she saw Marsha's chin going down, Carol cut her some slack and her confidence was bolstered when she intercepted a few passes. The whistle went and they headed to the benches for a quick drink break with the other women and girls.

'How's it going?' asked Rose.

'Great,' said Carol. 'She's a natural.'

Sasha nodded but Suzanne rolled her eyes like a teenager. Her younger sister Chardonnay passed her a ball. 'Good job you're not shooting tonight then, Suzanne. You wouldn't want to be shown up by a newbie.'

Suzanne's know it all look disappeared as the others laughed.

'I think we'll start with me and Penny shooting this end, with Sandy and Marsha in defence. Okay, Rose?' Carol could see the tension between Suzanne and Marsha. She knew it wouldn't take much for Marsha to throw the towel in.

'That's fine by me,' said Penny. 'I have to leave early tonight so I need to play with Carol so we're good for next week's match.'

'Have you got a hot date then, Penny?' asked Suzanne.

'Actually Paul's away, Suzanne, so no I haven't.'

Suzanne walked away, sniggering to herself. Penny went to follow but Carol tossed her a ball.

'Shall we get some practice in?'

35

Carol knew it wouldn't make much difference to the following week's match whether she practised with Penny tonight or not. She'd played Goal Attack to Penny's Goal Shooter for three seasons and both women knew each other's play instinctively. Penny assumed she'd be picked for the first team and unless someone had substituted Rose for a Doppelganger, she was absolutely right.

Rose seemed oblivious to anything but the netball. Believing it would be good for Marsha to mark Penny, she decided to umpire before playing so she could see any potential for herself.

'That's fine, Carol. Come on then, girls. Let's get on. A couple of ten minute sessions then I'll let you know the teams for next Tuesday's matches.' Their first team were due to play The Eagles and their second the Hawks, in the final matches before the end of the league. The summer league would start six weeks later but not all of the club members played in both leagues.

They stopped chatting, picked up their bibs and made their way onto court.

*****

Marsha was on a high when she returned home. Keith was out as usual but she told her mother-in-law all about her evening.

'You're very brave trying a new sport at your age.'

'I'm only thirty, Ann. Some of the women are in their early forties and a lot fitter than me. I'd say a few are even older but I didn't like to ask.'

'Do you think you're going to go back?'

'I'll see how I feel in the morning. Do you want some supper or have you eaten?'

'No I thought I'd wait. You can show me how to do that pasta and cheese dish again if you like?'

Marsha was knackered but they had to eat. 'Come on then.' She headed for the kitchen knowing she was already addicted to netball. Not even the likes of Rose and Suzanne could dampen her enthusiasm.

*****

Carol tried to talk Marsha into going to the match with them the following Tuesday but she declined. To arrive in time for the match, the players had to leave work half an hour early. The office workers were able to work flexi-time or take time off

36

in lieu, but the cleaners didn't have that option so would need to work part of their lunch hour. Their boss was flexible so they didn't have to work their lunch on the same day. Marsha hadn't been made aware of that, so thought her boss would be unhappy if both her and Suzanne took this option. She was the new girl and Suzanne had made sure she knew it was a case of last in first out. She'd also made it known that the others wouldn't tolerate anyone who was too big for their boots. Marsha hoped that by covering the last half hour in the day, they'd realise she was a team player and not listen to Suzanne, who seemed determined to stir up trouble.

*****

The match was fierce. The Panthers were marginally ahead after the first two quarters and Rose thought they were going to finish the third quarter ahead by two goals. Then Suzanne threw a bad pass. It was intercepted by the opposition Wing Defence who threw a quick ball to their Centre. Not fast enough to move from attack to defence, Sandy wasn't close enough to her player to intercept the ball when the Centre passed it to the Goal Attack. She jumped into the air to retrieve it and landed just inside the shooting circle. Seeing that Rose was tight on her Goal Shooter, the Goal Attack took a shot and scored. The whistle went and The Eagles jumped and shouted as if they'd won the match, not the quarter. Rose was fuming.

'That was a dreadful pass, Suzanne. What were you thinking?' she didn't wait for an answer. 'Scrub that, coz obviously you weren't thinking about netball.'

For once Suzanne didn't have a smart arse reply. She ran to the ladies obviously upset but Rose was oblivious.

'We've got to get this back. If we lose this match we're second in the league and stay in this division for another season.' It was only the winners who were promoted and Rose was desperate for that to be The Panthers.

Back on court for the fourth quarter The Eagles were hyped up and the momentum went with them for the first ten minutes. They stretched their lead to eight goals. Carol tried to motivate her team but their heads were already down and despite their best efforts it wasn't enough. They clawed back three goals but The Eagles won by five.

'Dream over for another year,' said Rose.

37

Carol tried to convince herself that nobody had died, but looking at her team, it certainly felt like they had. Most of them wandered off to make their way home. Nobody felt like going for an after match drink.

'I'm off too,' said Rose. 'Thanks for agreeing to umpire the next match for me, Carol. Gail will be here shortly.'

'Okay. See you at training tomorrow.' She watched as Rose left, head down and bitterly disappointed.

The second match involved their B team against the Hawks. Both teams were in a lower division and Carol expected it to be a scrappier match. Gail, their non-playing umpire and Deputy Head of the league arrived. They said their hellos and got their whistles, scorecards and pencils ready. Gail checked the nails of the players while Carol used the bathroom and they were ready to go on her return.

Within the first minute she noticed the Goal Attack for the Hawks. She was a teenager but Carol wasn't sure how old as the girl was tall. She was also very talented. She's a first team player thought Carol, as she wondered why the new girl wasn't playing for The Eagles. She hadn't seen her play before so the lass might have been new to the area. It would make sense that she would have to prove herself in the second team before moving up. But there was something vaguely familiar about her. She reminded Carol of someone but she couldn't quite put her finger on who. It'll come to me, she thought until the Jaguars Goal Defence contacted the new Goal Attack and Carol returned to the present.

'Contact. Penalty against you Goal Defence. Pass or shot.' The Goal Defence stood by her opponent's side and the Goal Attack took a shot at goal, but missed. She moved quickly to the post and grabbed the ball on the rebound. This time it hit its target. The Jaguars had expected an easy win but due in large part to the skill of the Hawks' new Goal Attack, lost their match by two goals. Not a whitewash but Rose wouldn't be happy. A loss for both teams wasn't an ideal way to end the season. Carol was glad there was an end of season tournament in three weeks where the league prizes would be presented and the less experienced players would have a chance to play in a match. She packed up her kit, congratulated the winners, commiserated with the losers, and made her way home.

Chapter 6

Paul had made his fortune by other people's misfortune and misery. He had a string of pawnbrokers and money-lending agencies and a recycling business. He employed area managers at each major location but liked to visit personally so still travelled all over the country.

Paul was more careful than his wife and the agency he used were discreet. The girls were professional and generally satisfied his needs. As far as he was concerned, it was a physical transaction and he didn't consider inviting any of them to stay overnight in his hotel rooms. Unable to erase the details of an email from his mind, Paul had sent tonight's girl away without fully satisfying himself, then opened his computer to re-read the message from his lawyer and friend, Brian. Brian had engaged the services of a private detective and Paul re-read the report. Penny had been seeing the same man for over six months. The Syrian. This one had lasted longer than any of the others. Could she actually be serious about him? He shook off that thought. There was only one person his wife loved. She thought she loved Kaitlyn but only when their daughter reminded her of herself. Paul made his way to the bathroom and took a long, hot shower. It helped him think clearly. The situation was worrying and the worst it had been during their twenty-year marriage. By the time he'd dried and put on his towelling robe, he'd made his decision. Pouring himself a whisky, he took a large gulp and made the call.

Brian answered on the second ring and Paul got straight to business.

'Offer him what?' Brian was astounded. 'What if he doesn't want to move to Scotland?'

'He will. Speak to some of our people and get him a job, but not in my businesses. Make sure he knows the consequences of turning down my offer.'

'Are you sure about this, Paul?' They'd been friends for years. Brian was one of a few people Paul trusted completely. He usually appreciated his frankness and honesty, but not today.

'Do it, Brian.'

'Will do.'

'Now to Penny. This time she's gone too far.'

Shall I stop part of her allowance?'

Paul arranged for a monthly allowance to be paid into his wife's bank account.

'No. I don't want her to be suspicious. Do some digging. I want to know what's the least I can give her as a settlement.'

'Under the circumstances, Paul, I think anything would be generous on your part.'

'My thoughts exactly,' he took a drink. 'Do you have the list of them all?'

'Yup.'

'I'm hoping that even Penny would be embarrassed for her own daughter to discover what she's been up to. That's my main bargaining chip.'

'And if she's not?'

'We take her to the cleaners anyway. I've had as much as I can stomach.'

'Got it. And what about Kaitlyn?' asked Brian.

'What about her?'

'Do I factor in anything Penny gives to Kaitlyn? You don't want your daughter to go without do you?'

'No need for that. I fund Kaitlyn's education but you know she has to fund her own lifestyle. She'll appreciate that when she's qualified and earning her own money.'

'I thought that. But last time I saw her she was wearing designer clothes and sporting an expensive handbag while she flashed the cash.' Paul had arranged for Kaitlyn to network with some junior lawyers during a function attended by the law company Brian co-owned.

'So what? You assumed that Penny was giving her an allowance behind my back?'

'No, Paul. I know she can get around you so assumed she could get around her mother too.'

Paul could hear the worry in his friend's voice. 'Something's not right here but you weren't to know.'

'Shall I get the PI onto it?'

Paul nodded to himself. Brian could read his mind at times.

'No. Let me think about that first.' It was one thing spying on his wife, but he trusted his beautiful daughter and that wouldn't seem right.

They hung up. He felt much better having made the decision he should have done years before, but needed a distraction to stop him worrying about Kaitlyn. He adored his daughter but was she as devious as her mother if it meant getting her own way?

Paul called the agency again; a girl would be with him in twenty minutes.

Chapter 7

'Are you going to training today?' Carol had arranged to meet Marsha for a light lunch in the self-service restaurant.

'Certainly am. I thought I could learn more during the break between the winter and summer leagues.'

Carol was pleasantly surprised. 'You like it then?'

'Understatement.' Marsha moved the bland salad around her plate, trying to work up some enthusiasm for the food. 'Look. I know I'm overweight and unfit but I think I'm going to really enjoy netball. It's good to get out of the house and forget what's going on there.'

'Your mother-in-law?'

'No, Carol. This is between us, isn't it?'

'You can trust me, Marsha, but don't tell me anything that makes you feel uncomfortable.'

'Thanks, but it's fine. I need to talk,' she pushed her plate away. 'If you'd told me a few months ago that my mother-in-law would turn into a good friend I would have laughed in your face, but that's what she is now. I wouldn't talk to her about Keith but now she's seen what's going on, I think she feels sorry for me.'

Carol gave an encouraging smile. 'Go on.'

'It's not only that. I think she was incredibly lonely and stuck in a rut. We go to bingo on Fridays and she's met some new friends there. One of them is an old bloke and I think they're striking up more than a friendship.' Marsha laughed to herself. 'She seems to have a new lease of life and doesn't make nasty comments to me like she used to.'

'That's great news. I know living with relatives can be really hard so it's good that you're getting on so well.' Carol knew there was more to it but didn't want to pry.

'You've probably guessed that Ann isn't the problem.'

'I thought there was something else.'

'It's Keith. The Keith you see in the bar and that Sam sees in work is different to the real man.'

'He doesn't hurt you does he?'

'He used to when he was drunk but that's stopped since we've lived with his mother. But he's cold, uncaring and controlling. He was such a catch and took me on at a difficult time in my life so I always thought I was unworthy. Something's

42

snapped, Carol. I knew early on he was a bad one but couldn't admit it to myself. But now it's like I can see the real Keith for the first time and I don't like what I'm seeing.'

'That doesn't sound good. Have you tried talking to him? Do you even want to sort things out?'

Marsha sighed. 'I have tried talking yes, but it's not as simple as that. We have lots of problems but whenever I try to discuss anything that's not to do with dinner or football, he either clams up or has a tantrum and goes out. He's out most nights and sometimes he stays out all night.'

'It sounds to me as if you could both do with some help. Have you thought about marriage guidance?'

Marsha gave a sardonic laugh. 'No way. There's more chance of me being abducted by aliens than him agreeing to that.'

'I see. Is there anything I can help with?'

'You have helped by just listening. Thanks, Carol.'

'That's what friends do.'

'I know, but I do appreciate it. I'm not ready to give up on twelve years of marriage just yet but I wonder if it's worth the effort anymore. Anyway,' she started putting the crockery on the tray to return to the trolley, 'I'll be too knackered at netball training to think about my problems so that's a good thing.' She looked at her watch. 'Oh shit, is that the time. I'd better get back before Suzanne tries to get one over on me and grasses me up for being late. I still don't know why she hates me so much.'

They left the table and said goodbye to Sasha who was talking to one of her staff. 'I shouldn't take it personally, Marsha. Suzanne seems to dislike most people.'

'Well that's made me feel a little better at least.'

They linked arms and made their way back to the offices, Carol to work at her desk and Marsha to clean the rooms and floors along the North corridor.

*****

Even though the main season was over, many players carried on training. The first team was still upset that they came second in the league and most were determined to win the tournament. Rose took defeat personally. Suzanne had assumed she was over it by now.

'Chardonnay, do the warm up please then we'll split into three groups. Come on, let's get going, we're here to play netball.' Rose was all business. She was fed up with the players talking

43

about their personal lives when they were supposed to be training. The women followed Chardonnay but kept chatting until the warm-up became more strenuous. They stopped after twenty minutes. Rose took a quick drink then spoke.

'Today I want to go right back to basics. Firstly, The Jaguars and less experienced players need to practise their passes, and footwork drills. Carol can you take the girls down the other end of the court please?'

'Okay. Grab some balls then ladies, one between two.' Carol headed off with the second team and new players.

'Everyone else form two lines, we'll start with some basic drills. We need two feeders. Good of you to join us Sandy,' she turned to the latecomer. 'For God's sake! You're almost half an hour late. How difficult is it to get here on time?'

'Sorry, Rose.'

Sandy started warming up, wondering who or what had put Rose in such a bad mood.

'Suzanne, where are you going?'

'Err, I was going to feed, along with Chardonnay.'

'Actually, Suzanne, I want you to go back to basics with Carol's group. You could do with practising your passing.'

'Because I made one bad pass last week?!'

The others could see where this was heading so stopped talking amongst themselves.

'Your passing cost us the match and it wasn't only once. You got pulled up for footwork as well. Too many basic errors.'

'You never had a bad day, Rose?'

'Of course. But never that bad that it cost us the league.'

'So it's all my fault?' Suzanne was trying to keep her temper in check.

Knowing her sister as she did, Chardonnay thought it time to intervene.

'It wasn't all down to Suzanne, Rose. It could have gone either way and we were just unlucky.'

'I know that, but Suzanne still had a sloppy game and needs to practice her passing and footwork. Go and join the others, Suzanne.'

'Not bloody likely.' She threw the ball to the floor with such force that it bounced high into the air. She had no intention of catching or retrieving it. 'You know what you can do with your netball club, Rose?'

44

Rose could guess.

'You can shove it where the sun don't shine, you stuck up controlling...'

'That's enough, Suzanne,' said Chardonnay but her sister was already retrieving her kit.

'I'm going to play for a club where I'm appreciated and can have a laugh. I'll flaming show you.' She grabbed her bag and headed for the exit. Chardonnay rushed after her, trying to stop her sister but Suzanne shrugged her off.

'Okay. Show's over, let's get on,' said Rose as if nothing had happened.'

Chardonnay headed back to the group. 'That was unfair, Rose.' Not many of the players would question Rose's authority, even the adults, so the others were impressed that Chardonnay was willing to stick up for her sister. She was more mature than Suzanne, even though almost five years younger.

'I don't think so, but we'll have a chat later.' Chardonnay knew she was wasting her time so picked up a ball and started the drill. She had no intention of leaving the club but would be able to tell Suzanne that she'd tried to defend her, even though Rose wasn't interested. Chardonnay planned to go to the flat her sister shared with her boyfriend, straight after training.

Later, Rose split the players into equal teams and asked Carol and Chardonnay to umpire. Although Chardonnay wasn't qualified she knew the rules and wanted to become an umpire when she was older. With practise and encouragement, Rose knew she'd be good. She decided to stay off for the first session so she could assess the players. They were supposed to field two teams of equal ability for the tournament but Rose wanted to ensure they won, so would have to box clever.

Marsha was coming on in leaps and bounds and Carol was pleased for her new friend. She was like a sponge and absorbed all new information quickly. As Carol watched, she forgot for a moment that she was supposed to be umpiring.

'Carol,' called Chardonnay from the other side of the court. 'Do you want me to take the toss-up?'

She'd missed the offence and the youngster was covering for her. 'Sorry, girls. I was miles away there,' she laughed. 'Promise I'll pay more attention.' She took the toss-up and the session continued. Carol tried to concentrate but realising who Marsha reminded her of, hit her like a punch to the guts. It wasn't purely coincidence. She struggled to pay attention until the session ended but made a few wrong decisions.

'You looked distracted,' said Rose when Carol blew the whistle a few minutes before the agreed fifteen minutes. 'Try to concentrate. Please.'

Although Rose wasn't as sharp as she would have been with some of the others, it still irked Carol but she decided to let it go. 'Yeah, just need the bathroom. Won't be a mo.'

She locked herself in a cubicle and sat down. So the new young Goal Attack in the Hawks team played in the same way as Marsha. So what? she asked herself. But it wasn't only the way she played. She was tall, like Marsha and their mannerisms were the same, from the way Marsha threw her head back when she laughed to the way she put her hair behind her ear when she was nervous. The voice nagging in her head had been answered and it was definitely Marsha that the girl reminded her of. Not in looks but many other ways. Could they be sisters? Marsha had told her she didn't have any family. Could there be more to it? Carol knew there was more to her friend than met the eye and wondered if she could broach the subject. She remembered how she felt when going through a major change in her own life and decided that now wasn't the time to speak to Marsha. They would see the other players at the tournament and that would give Carol a chance to have a better look, and to see her friend's reaction.

After a few more sessions they did a cool down, put the equipment away until the following week, and headed home.

*****

Brian called Sayid and arranged a meeting in an out of town hotel. When Sayid arrived he introduced himself and told the Syrian to follow him.

'Where are we going?' It wasn't every day you met the lawyer who worked for your lover's husband and he was rightly nervous.

'To a room. This is private business and I don't want to be overheard. Don't look so worried.'

His smile didn't convince Sayid, but curiosity got the better of him and he followed anyway. The room was large and had a separate lounge with a settee, small table and two comfortable looking chairs. Brian indicated where Sayid should sit and poured himself a drink.

'Drink?' he asked.

46

When his guest declined he took some paperwork out of his bag.

'Read this.'

The Syrian looked up after a while. 'Let me get this straight. Penelope's husband is willing to put a deposit down on a house for me and has got me a job so that I'll be able to pay the mortgage?'

'Exactly.'

'But I have to relocate my family,' he shook the paper. 'To Scotland?'

'That's right, yes.'

'And if I refuse?'

'I'm sure you'll agree Mr Mason's offer is more than generous.' Brian didn't wait for an answer. 'But if you refuse he can, and will, make your life very difficult.'

'Are you threatening me?'

Brian grabbed the neck of Sayid's jacket with both hands and lifted him off the chair. He pushed him so that his head banged the wall. Not loosening his grip, Brian's head was inches from the Syrian's.

'Listen, you fucking scumbag. You're lucky that Mr Mason doesn't want to kill you and dispose of your body so that nobody will ever find it. If he'd taken my advice that's exactly what would have happened. So yes, I am threatening you.' He let go and the smaller man edged back to the chair and sat down. He thought he loved Penelope but had just discovered he loved money and life even more.

'Where do I sign?'

'That's more like it.' Brian pointed to the crosses he'd already marked on the paper. 'If you talk about this or tell anyone about you and Penelope this contract will become null and void and you will disappear. Evidence will show your family that you have gone to fight the cause and they and any friends you might have will be hounded by the authorities and disgraced. Do I make myself clear.'

'Absolutely.' He couldn't control his shaking hand as he signed the papers. After he'd finished, Brian held out his hand to shake as if to seal a friendly legitimate deal. Sayid had no intention of winding him up and shook without hesitation.

47

Chapter 8

Penny walked from room to room in the mansion, bored out of her brain. She was even tired of shopping and was surprised the first time she'd tried to call Sayid; a voice said the number didn't exist. A bottle and a half of wine later, she'd lost count of the times she'd dialled his number. Her brain knew it was over but she refused to believe he would end it without even telling her. Penny looked at the red liquid in the glass. She threw it and watched in fascination as it hit the American-style fridge. The pieces shattered and the wine eventually ended up in puddles on the soft cream floor tiles. Staggering to the lounge, she crashed onto the settee and screamed as she punched the cushions.

'How dare he, how dare he.' Her anger vented, she sat up and looked to the ceiling. 'Nobody does this to me, Sayid. I'll find you and make you pay.'

She got up and slowly made her way upstairs, her rejected and drunken mind intent on revenge, even though she had no idea how.

*****

Chardonnay hadn't seen her sister since she'd left netball training in a strop. Nobody was home when she'd called round to her flat so she assumed her boyfriend Dean must have taken her out to console her. Suzanne hadn't turned up to training the following week and Chardonnay had been busy with her friends and studies. She felt guilty and knew Suzanne would have a go at her, but she was still her sister and nine days was a long time to go without hearing from her. Their mother was beginning to worry, as Suzanne hadn't returned her calls either.

'Will you go and see her on your way to India's, love?'

Chardonnay said she would and left early.

There was no answer when she knocked on the door but she could hear Dolly Parton singing so someone had to be home. Deciding to stay until the door was answered, she banged it three times.

'I know someone's in,' she shouted. 'Come on, Suzanne. Answer the flaming door.'

The music stopped and the door opened shortly after. Suzanne popped her head around it. Chardonnay's first thought was that she looked like a panda.

'O.M.G! What's happened?'

'Come in,' Suzanne opened the door wide enough for her sister to squeeze through. The inside was in semi-darkness, the curtains closed and the air stale. Dirty crockery was piled up in the sink and the coffee table festooned with mugs, glasses and plates. The remains of breakfast was in one dish, an uneaten sandwich on a plate and the dregs of red wine was in a glass.

'O.M.G! What's going on, Suzanne? Are you okay?'

'Will you stop saying *O.M.G* for Christ sake. You're doing my head in.'

'Well look at the state of you and this place. What do you expect me to say?'

Chardonnay expected them to get into a full-blown argument. They could argue over fresh air and she wondered if they would ever get along. Her sister surprised her.

'Dean's left me.'

'O.M... Oh no. You poor thing. I'm so sorry, Suzanne.' She stepped towards her sister to hug her, but Suzanne stepped away.

'It's okay, he's a boring sod anyway. I'm all right.'

'Well you don't look all right. And what's with all the mess? It looks like your room used to but this place is always clean.'

'Bloody hell, Chardonnay. I tell you my boyfriend's left and all you care about is the state of my flat. We're not all flaming perfect. Okay?'

'I'm not saying anyone's perfect, Suzanne, I'm just surprised because your flat always looks lovely and I thought you'd turned over a new leaf.'

'If you must know, Dean is really good at cooking, cleaning and all that shit and I just leave him to it. I'll have to get used to doing it all myself until my new fella moves in.' She gathered the plates and glasses off the coffee table and headed for the kitchen.

'You've got a new fella? So you cheated on Dean and that's why he left?'

'Oh for fuck's sake, Chardonnay! You know nothing about being an adult and living with someone. Don't be so judgemental.'

'But...'

'But nothing. I'm not in the mood for this. Get out, go on.' She started pushing her sister towards the door.

49

'But who's your new fella and what will I tell Mum and Dad?'

'Tell them Dean's left and as soon as my fella leaves his wife he'll be moving in with me.'

'O.M.G! Seriously...'

'See ya, Chardonnay. Good to chat.'

Chardonnay jumped into the corridor to dodge the slamming door. She phoned India as she ran down the stairs, explaining to her friend that she had period pains and was feeling too rough to come over. She would tell her best friend everything but needed to tell her parents first. Even though it wasn't her place, Chardonnay hated to think of them hearing the news from one of the local gossips.

*****

Marsha had been dreading work that Friday. Suzanne was still trying to turn the others against her and had been her usual horrible self the day before. Marsha had no idea why her colleague had it in for her. How could the girl sing like an angel but act like a demon? If Suzanne spent as much time working as she did bitching or stirring she would win glowing praise from her bosses. Fortunately her niggly comments and snide remarks appeared to have the opposite effect of what she'd intended. Carol had overheard Lil telling Suzanne to give it a rest when criticising Marsha. Suzanne had alienated more than one of her colleagues but instead of easing off on Marsha, it had made her worse.

As it was, Friday turned out to be a much better day than expected. Firstly, Lil told her that Suzanne had phoned in sick. Result thought Marsha, knowing that work-wise, nobody would notice. At the first morning break Sandy popped into the staff room.

'Hi ladies. Marsha, can you spare me a minute please?' she beckoned and Marsha followed her outside.

'Can you come up to the restaurant office? Sasha wants to see you.'

'Okay, but Mr Sutton's office is next on my list and he's a bit fussy. Can I clean his first? And why does she want to see me?'

Sandy laughed. 'Don't worry. Wait here and I'll have a quick word with Lil. Sasha said it was important.'

After arranging for Lil to clean Mr Sutton's office, Sandy and Marsha walked to the self-service restaurant. It was

50

almost ten-thirty and coming towards the end of NAAFI Break for the soldiers who were still lucky enough to have a morning break. Marsha blushed as one of the youngsters winked at her.

'Behave yourself,' said another, before looking at her. 'Take no notice of the idiot, love,' he smiled at her and Marsha blushed for a totally different reason.

'Don't call me an idiot, Gary...'

Sandy laughed and pretended to cuff the winker as they passed. Sasha's door was open and she asked Marsha to go straight in.

'Thanks, Sandy. You've saved me a bit of time.' As Sandy said her goodbyes Sasha gave a big sigh and took her eyes away from the monitor. She explained that they were short-staffed in the restaurant. 'Two are on maternity leave and one of the girls has to have an operation on her back. She's going to be off for quite a while.'

'I'm sorry to hear that, sounds like a nightmare.'

'It certainly is, and that's where you come in.'

'Me?'

Sasha could see she hadn't figured it out. 'You've only been with us for a short time but I've heard nothing but good reports about you and your work. Excellent in fact.'

Marsha blushed for the third time that morning.

'So I want to train you up to work in the restaurant. You'll serve the food, clean the tables, work on the tills and any other jobs that need doing. What do you think?'

'I'm not sure. I haven't done anything like this before and I quite like my cleaning job.'

'Okay. But it's almost eight pound a week more than you're already earning, for the same hours.'

'That means I'll be earning about the same as Keith. I think I might be interested.' She laughed but stopped when she saw Sasha's confused look.

'I think you're mistaken. The drivers are on more money than the cleaning and restaurant staff.' When Marsha looked doubtful, she emphasised her point. 'Barry worked here for a while and his starting pay was a lot better and that was a few years ago.'

'Oh, sorry. I must have been mistaken.'

'No problem,' Sasha doubted Marsha would confront her lying husband. It was none of her business so she returned to the

51

original matter. 'So I'll draw up your contract, get you some uniforms and you can start on Monday if that suits.'

It was a big step but would mean she wouldn't have to work with Suzanne. She wanted to confirm this before accepting. 'Are any of the other cleaners being offered a job in here?'

'The ladies who have been asked in the past are happy staying where they are. There is one who wants to work here but she's not suitable at the moment.'

Marsha hoped it wasn't Suzanne. 'Then I'd love to start on Monday. Thanks, Sasha, I'm looking forward to it already.'

Had she not discovered that Keith had been lying about his wages, Marsha would have been walking on air. As it was, she doubted he'd admit to lying and it would cause more harm than good to have it out with him. Work and netball had opened up another world. She was losing weight and gaining confidence. The voice in her head told her that she did deserve a better life. It also told her to go to the bank and open a savings account in her own name. Keith knew all about her current account so she needed one he didn't know about. They finished early on Fridays so using her new mobile phone Marsha called her mother-in-law to explain that she was popping into town do so some shopping.

'I could do with a bit of fresh air,' said Ann. 'So I'll meet you there.'

Marsha reckoned she'd have enough time to go to the bank before meeting Ann outside the supermarket.

Ann spoke first. 'Keith phoned just before I left to say he's working late and won't be home for his tea. He's going straight out from work and has lost your new number that's why he phoned me.'

'Fine.'

'What are you really thinking, love?'

They didn't have heart to heart conversations so the question threw her. Ann had recently started to openly disapprove of her son's behaviour, so she decided to be honest.

'He won't talk to me, hardly ever eats with us and stays out all night whenever he wants,' she sighed. 'So I'm thinking there's not much hope for our marriage.'

'Do you still love him?'

'You're his mother, Ann, I'm not...'

'I love him because he's my son. But I don't like him.'

52

'Do you think he's found someone else?' Marsha asked. She could see the answer in her mother-in-law's face.

'Every marriage has its ups and downs. But I didn't realise how he really treated you until you came to live with me.'

'You must have realised, Ann, when you came to stay with us? Didn't you notice the way he talked to me?'

'I'm so sorry, Marsha.' She put her hand on her daughter-in-law's forearm and stopped to look at her. Ann was trying to speak but the words wouldn't come.

'Shall we go somewhere quiet for a drink so we can have a proper talk?'

Ann simply nodded so Marsha led them both to the nearest pub. It was doing reasonable trade but was too early for the Friday evening rush, so they found a private corner booth. Ann hadn't been to a pub in ages but needed a drink.

'What would you like?'

'Babycham please, that's if they sell them.'

Marsha had never heard of the drink. The barman laughed when she ordered one for each of them and said he'd bring them to the table.

'Keith's father died when he was five so he's been my life ever since.'

'That must have been awful for you and Keith. But it's such a long time ago. Did you ever think of meeting someone else to share your life with?'

It was as if the floodgates had opened and Ann couldn't stop talking. She explained that she'd suffered with agoraphobia and had found it difficult to go outside after her husband's death. She'd had to because of Keith but as he grew up, she'd depended on him more and more.

'Then he met you and moved away. It was so hard, Marsha, but I knew I had to make the effort if I wanted to see my son. I resented you.'

'But why didn't you talk to me?'

'Well you weren't willing to visit me, so I assumed you disliked me and didn't see the point of talking about it.'

'What?'

Seeing the surprise on Marsha's face confused Ann. Surely Keith hadn't lied all of these years? The penny quickly dropped.

'Keith told me early on that you refused to come to my house. Why do you think I was so off with you?'

'Oh, Ann. So it took everything for you to travel to see your son. All the while you thought I didn't like you enough to visit. How awful. No wonder...'

'You were going to say no wonder I was such a cow.'

Despite the revelations, they both laughed.

'Now we know the truth, what are we going to do about it?' Ann asked.

'You know if I try to talk to him about this he'll throw me out?'

'It's my house, Marsha and I won't let him. There's no way...'

'He's your son, Ann, despite what I think of him. He would never forgive you for taking my side in this over his.'

'But...'

'But nothing.'

They sat in silence, each wondering what to do for the best.

'I don't want you to move out. Now that we've become friends...' said Ann, her words tapering off.

'I know we hardly see him these days, but can you trust yourself not to say anything, knowing the hurt he's caused us both?'

'I can if you can.'

'It's a deal,' said Marsha.

'And anyway, don't tell Keith this either but I've already got enough on my plate. I've been having counselling and the panic attacks happen less often. The counsellor told me to avoid stressful situations as much as I can.'

'Oh, Ann.' She moved and gave her mother-in-law a hug. Ann returned the embrace.

'It's much better now that you're living with me. I didn't realise how sad and lonely I was.'

'Even though Keith...'

'Yes,' Ann interrupted. 'I know he's my son but I also know he's a total bastard.'

Ann felt like a naughty girl and they both laughed.

'Promise me that whatever happens between you, that you'll stay with me, Marsha.'

'I can't promise that.'

'But...'

'Ann. I can't promise that because if the worst happens between us I know Keith will kick me out. It won't be my choice but that's how it is.'

'Over my dead body,' said Ann then gulped down the last of her Babycham.

'Whatever your son's done, I don't want to come between you.'

'I'll deal with that if and when the time comes but let's make sure that's not anytime soon.'

'Agreed.'

'But believe me when I say it's my house and what I say goes. Now let's have another one of these and shall we eat out tonight?'

'What a good idea, then I can tell you all about my new job. And shall I order a bottle of Prosecco instead? The girls at netball rave about the stuff and I'm dying to try it.'

Marsha headed for the bar, the only cloud in her sunny life was her husband, but unbeknown to her, that cloud was soon to be lifted.

*****

Before embarking on his next string of visits, Paul had arranged a quick meeting with Brian at the pawnbrokers in Bloomington town. A bulky black man was standing at the counter discussing a necklace and matching earrings with the assistant. Paul watched discreetly as the assistant asked the manager for help.

'How did you come to own these pieces?' asked the manager.

'They belonged to my wife's family and were passed down to my wife,' said the man. 'We need the money more than the jewellery so she is happy to get rid of them.'

'Hmm.' The manager held the jewellery up to the light and studied it. 'So the origin of these pieces is?'

'Fiji.'

'And you have the paperwork to prove it?'

'No I don't. They're very old.'

'I see. Take a seat, I won't keep you waiting for long.'

The manager went through to the back and was joined by Paul and Brian. The jewellery was of European origin, which was obvious to all three. They wouldn't touch it with a bargepole.

'He must be desperate for the money,' said Brian who exchanged a knowing look with Paul.

'Ask him to come through, Mal,' Paul said to the manager. 'Then leave us to it.'

Mal had no idea what was going on but left as instructed. 'He could fit the bill,' said Paul. 'You speak to him and make the arrangements. I don't want him to know who I am. And find out where the jewellery came from so we have something on him too, and there's no chance it'll backfire.'

Paul left by the back door.

*****

Penny was on her way to Greens in the Mall to pick up some chocolate. As she walked she scrolled through her contact list, hoping to make arrangements for a girlie lunch the following week. She didn't see the man and they walked right into each other. She dropped her phone.

'Oops,' he said as he bent to retrieve it. 'Are you all right, love?'

He had the same sort of accent as some of the Fijian netball girls and a pleasant smile. But what was most noticeable to Penny was his body. He wore a t-shirt without a jacket, even though there was a chill in the air, and tight fitting jeans.

'I think I'm fine thanks,' Penny eyed him like a lion picking its next meal. 'Actually, I feel a bit faint,' she put her hand to her head and stumbled. The man took hold of her arm and led her to a nearby bench.

'Ooh, sorry about that, I think I need a coffee.' She got up from the bench and faltered, looking like a B Movie actress.

'Shall I help you?' asked Leon.

'I feel so silly, but would you mind?'

Leon said it would be his pleasure and Penny led them towards the coffee shop. He hesitated at the door.

'Would you like to join me for a coffee?' she asked. He looked unsure so she persisted. 'As a small thank you for your inconvenience.'

'It was no bother at all, but yes, why not.'

She introduced herself and so did Leon. It didn't occur to him to use a different name.

'I couldn't help noticing that you sound Fijian. Do you work on the base, in the Army?'

'No, I'm in the Air Force,' it was the first thought that came into his head. 'I'm based in Yorkshire but we're here for a few weeks to train some soldiers.'

'I see,' said Penny. 'Maybe we could meet up again, for coffee?' The way she touched his arm and smiled made it obvious that it wasn't coffee she was after. 'Before you return to Yorkshire?'

Leon returned the smile. 'Why not?'

They exchanged numbers. She knew she was taking a risk by seeing someone who worked on the base, but couldn't envisage major problems as she only used the base for netball and Leon was a short-term visitor.

He called the following day and Penny suggested a hotel in the city where they could meet for a meal.

'I'm not sure I can...'

'On me, Leon. As a thank you.'

They hung up and Sayid was already becoming a distant memory as she licked her lips in anticipation of their meeting.

*****

Kaitlyn had one last week before leaving uni for the summer holidays. After spending a few weeks at home, she planned to go away with Evie. Her parents had already paid for the hotel but as part of her *know the value of money* training, decided she had to earn her own spending money. She took all the jobs she could get that final week so she could enjoy her holiday to the full.

Two nights before she was due to break up, the agency called telling her to go to a five-star country hotel, which was twenty miles out of town. She also received explicit instructions about what to wear. The taxi there and back was already paid so she put the finishing touches to her hair and make up and left the flat she shared with Evie. During the journey Kaitlyn wondered what the driver would think if he knew she only had a basque and suspenders on under her camelhair coat. She already had the room number on arrival at the hotel, so made her way to the top floor. She smiled when she realised it was the penthouse suite – this one must be very rich.

She knocked on the door and waited. It opened and she was unsure which one of them was the most shocked.

57

'Daddy! Surprise!' He was in a thick white towelling robe so she embraced him, knowing he wouldn't be able to feel what she was wearing under her coat.

Paul said nothing at first, but his mind was working overtime.

'Kaitlyn I...' he opened the door wider. 'Come on in, darling. How did you find out I was here?' *This would be a good one.*

'Us girls have our ways and means, Daddy. I miss you soooooo much.' She kissed his cheek.

'Do you want some champagne, darling?'

'That would be lovely, were you expecting company?' As she walked towards the window Kaitlyn thought she'd got away with it. She'd managed to mask the shock on her face before her father noticed. It had been a very lucky escape. She didn't realise he was right behind her and before she had a chance to do anything about it, he pulled the back of her coat with such force that the buttons popped and the coat fell to her waist.

'Daddy!' she pulled the coat back up and turned to face him but had to look away when she saw his disgust.

'You slut!' The words were accompanied by a slap to her face. The first time her father had ever hit her. Kaitlyn screamed in pain and shock as her hand flew to her stinging cheek.

'Well it was you who said I had to work,' she shouted, while jabbing her finger at his chest.

Paul took hold of his daughter's wrists and forced her to keep still. 'I wanted you to take some responsibility and know what it is to work for your money. Not to become some high-class whore. Like mother like daughter, only your mother has a liking for more exotic men.' Paul turned and headed for the bathroom.

'Don't you dare! I'm not a whore and neither is Mummy. And I wouldn't have a job if it wasn't for men like you.'

Paul rinsed his face with cold water and looked in the mirror. He was devastated and disgusted but couldn't face the thought of a life without his daughter in it. She needed to be brought back in to the fold. He returned to the bedroom. His little girl had put her coat back on and was crying.

'Life is different for men, Kaitlyn.'

'I can see I've hurt you, Daddy, but if you really believe that, you're a hypocrite and we are as bad as each other.'

'This is what's going to happen. You will not return to York University after the summer break. I will arrange your transfer and you will get a proper job and you will most definitely behave. Do not think you can do anything behind my back, I will know your every move.'

'You can't make me do that.'

'You know damn well I can, Kaitlyn.'

'What if I refuse?'

'You are this close,' he showed her a tiny gap between his thumb and forefinger, 'to being disowned by me. If you refuse to go along with my instructions consider yourself disinherited, physically, emotionally and financially.'

No longer crying, Kaitlyn tried a different tack. 'Mummy would be upset and outraged if she knew what you are really like.'

'Your mother sleeps with other men,' he banged his fist on the wall. 'If your mother wasn't like she is, I wouldn't need to do this.'

'Mummy and other men? No way. Mummy's not like that.' Kaitlyn knew her mother was far too fussy to have casual sex.

'Yes. And not just one man either. And don't you ever mention any of this to your mother. I have plans.'

The last sounded sinister and for the first time in her life, Kaitlyn realised just how powerful her father really was.

'Now get out of my sight, you disgust me.'

'And you make me sick,' she whispered.

As she made her way out of the hotel, her father had already necked half a bottle of whisky. His little girl had turned from princess to whore. He knew it would take a lot more whisky before he could reach a place where his heart wasn't torn to pieces.

Chapter 9

Kaitlyn arrived home on the Thursday before the tournament.

'Darling, what a lovely surprise,' said Penny. 'I didn't expect you until tomorrow.' They kissed on both cheeks.

'I had a free day tomorrow so decided to come early. Is Daddy home?'

'I'm really sorry, darling but he phoned to say he's not going to make it. There's an issue with the business, which will take a few weeks to sort out. He said he'll help you move as soon as you're home from your holiday.'

'Great. What's for supper?'

'Maureen's made curry, cottage pie and a salad. She wasn't sure what you'd fancy. It just needs heating up.'

'Will you nuke the curry for me, Mummy while I go and get changed?'

'For goodness sake, Kaitlyn,' Penny tapped a short manicured nail on the breakfast bar. 'You're supposed to be a grown-up now. Can't you learn to do anything for yourself?'

'Pardon me for breathing,' said Kaitlyn as she disappeared up the stairs.

Penny took the packet of cigarettes out of a drawer and headed for the summerhouse. She sat on the bench outside, but still under cover. Lighting up she took a deep drag. She didn't smoke very often but now felt the need. Her daughter's appearance usually had this effect on her.

Returning to the house and feeling better with nicotine in her bloodstream, Penny decided to push the boat out and make an effort. By the time Kaitlyn reappeared, the plates, cutlery and serviettes were laid out on the breakfast bar, together with two glasses.

'The curry won't be long, darling. Prosecco?'

'Yes please.'

Penny popped the cork as the microwave pinged. 'Pour the drinks, darling while I see to the curry.'

Kaitlyn did as directed and a few minutes later they were tucking into their supper.

'Well this is fun,' said Penny. 'I hate to spoil the party, darling but it was quite a shock when your father told me you want to move to Surrey Uni. I thought you were happy at York.'

Kaitlyn remembered her father's warning. 'I was, Mummy. I mean I am. But I had a bit of trouble with a boy...'

'Why didn't you tell me, darling? Did he hurt you? Are you all right?'

'That's why I didn't tell you. I knew you'd worry and there was no need. I'm all right, really. He came into my room uninvited but before he could do me any real harm my friend sounded the alarm. Thank goodness she heard me screaming.'

'Oh, darling, how awful.' Penny wasn't very tactile with her family but gave Kaitlyn an embrace. It was awkward for them both but her daughter appreciated the sentiment and was happy her mother believed the story so far.

'It shook me up a bit and I have flashbacks. When I spoke to Daddy about it, he thought a change of scenery would help me.'

'And is that what you think, Kaitlyn?'

'I think it's best for everyone. And I'll be closer so will be able to come home at weekends.'

Penny hoped she still looked sympathetic. Despite her daughter's lucky escape, she didn't want her home at the weekends. She should be with people her own age.

'If that's all right with you?' Kaitlyn added.

'Of course, darling. This is your home and you're free to come and go as you please,' she took a sip of the Prosecco. 'Hmm, this is delicious. Shall we watch a film after dinner? A chic-flick or do you fancy something else?'

'I'm sorry, Mummy but I'm meeting some of the girls and going out.'

'Maybe I'll come with you?'

Kaitlyn's expression was one of horror.

'Only joking, darling. Have you any plans for tomorrow?'

'I've arranged to meet Kim and Louise so will be out for most of the day after breakfast.'

'Ah, okay. Maureen's in first thing so will make you whatever you want.' Penny was grateful her daughter was meeting old school friends so she wouldn't have to change her plans for the following day.

'But I'm definitely playing in the tournament on Saturday, so we'll be together all day then.'

'Of course we will, darling. Have fun tonight.'

61

'I will.'

Penny started to load the dishes into the dishwasher, knowing that it wouldn't occur to her spoilt daughter to do so. Kaitlyn got her coat and told her mother she'd see her the following day. As the door closed she forgot about Kaitlyn and shivered in anticipation of her own meeting the next day. Unable to contact Sayid, Penny knew it was time to move on. He was the first one who'd ignored her and initially she had been furious. After a few weeks she told herself the only way to get over it was to get back on the bus; not that Penny had ever ridden a bus in her adult life. She giggled to herself. Instead of seeking out a new companion – as she liked to think of them - at the club, bumping into Leon had presented the ideal opportunity.

She decided after two years of using *The Royal* hotel, it was time for a change. Leon was so big that his presence would stand out. It would be better therefore to try somewhere new where it was busier and he wouldn't cause any unwarranted stares. She wouldn't allow them to be seen together but knew there would be more anonymity in the capital. Penny made her way to *The Savoy* the following day. It didn't occur to her that he might feel uncomfortable in such plush surroundings. She checked in and phoned Leon from her suite, giving directions on how to get there. He arrived shortly after. Despite Penny lying on the bed in a state of undress, Leon was limp when he removed his pants. She looked at his face then his penis in disappointment. He shrugged his shoulders.

'It takes a lot of blood to wake this baby, but when he is awake...' he smiled. 'He ran his limp penis from her bellybutton up to her breasts. Penny closed her eyes, enjoying the feeling of it going from flaccid to erect. And what an erection!

'Oh my...' she was amazed when she opened her eyes. This was going to hurt. She grabbed his face and they kissed. Leon soon matched her passion and not much later, he was on top of her. Working from her neck down, his hands explored her body. Then he did the same with his tongue, until Penny could stand it no longer. He didn't need to ask if she was ready and she cried out as he pushed himself inside her.

There was no talk after they finished. Leon immediately fell asleep. Penny pondered that his equipment was certainly bigger than Sayid's and he was a good lover, but he didn't have the finesse or the exquisite skills of her previous companion. She would keep him for the time being but didn't envisage anything long-term. Still naked, she nodded off and didn't stir when he moved. He took the photographs as instructed, then instead of putting his phone away, he put it on record and placed it under the bed. When Leon got back into bed, she'd turned over with her back to him so he started fondling her breasts. Penny groaned then turned to face him. They made love again. After they finished she used the bathroom and he quickly stopped the recording on his phone and popped it into his jacket pocket. She returned and instructed him to take a shower.

'Later. I want to spend more time with you.'

She smiled. So he could be romantic and her magic had worked. He had already fallen for her.

'Go now, Leon. I have a surprise for you.'

He hid his annoyance and did as told, reminding himself that this was simply another duty.

Penny wondered if a Rolex watch was the right sort of present for such a burly man but it was too late now. She presented him with the gift before he left and he was delighted.

They said their goodbyes shortly after.

Leon found a dealer who would give him a decent amount of cash in exchange for the watch. This was a good, fun way of making the extra money his family needed and he was being paid by both parties. As he emailed Brian the photographs and details of the meeting, he didn't envisage it being a long-term relationship either.

He deleted Brian's acknowledgement and reminded himself to delete the photographs and the recording; he would but not just yet. They would come in handy during the graveyard shift on duties, when he was alone and unable to sleep.

*****

Marsha was all keyed up ready for the tournament. Keith had stayed out the night before but he wasn't even on her mind as she tried to visualise herself intercepting balls from the Goal Shooter she would mark. Her main aim was not to make an idiot of herself. She'd already been to the toilet twice that morning and felt she needed to go again. Ann shouted from downstairs.

'Your friend's car has just pulled up. Come on, love.' When she saw the look on Marsha's face as she headed down the stairs Ann laughed. 'Nobody's died, love and it's not the world cup. Go and enjoy yourself, you'll be fine.'

63

She decided not to add her opinion about grown women running around wearing short skirts and throwing balls at each other. Marsha looked nervous enough as it was. It wouldn't have happened in her day, but Ann knew the world was changing and she couldn't keep up with it.

A horn beeped outside.

'Good luck, love. See you later.'

Marsha brushed an imaginary piece of fluff off her light purple and navy trim skirt and picked up her sports bag. 'Thanks, Ann. See you later.' She took a deep breath and left the house.

'Hi, Carol.' She jumped in the passenger seat.

Carol said hello and told her they were collecting Chardonnay on the way. 'We'll see if there's any news about Suzanne. Nobody's seen her since she fell out with Rose.'

'I know, and she hasn't been in work either. I have to admit, it's made my life easier.'

They chatted easily and Carol noticed Marsha had temporarily forgotten about her pre-tournament nerves.

Chardonnay switched off as soon as Carol asked after Suzanne. 'Is she playing for any of the other teams today?'

'No, she's still poorly.' Chardonnay had no idea where her sister was but her mother had told her not to tell anyone. 'Have you lost more weight, Marsha?'

Marsha smiled, Chardonnay was such a sweetie.

They arrived at the tournament location; a high school with two outside courts and a large gymnasium with two inside courts in case of bad weather. There were sixteen teams, three of which were from the Bloomington Barracks club. It was meant to be a fun, end of season tournament with clubs agreeing to enter teams of equal ability. After losing the league, Rose was determined to win the tournament but knew she couldn't put all her first-team players into one team. By putting a few of the second team players along with the first-team netballers, Rose was able to convince herself and other club members that all was fair and square. Nobody in Bloomington would argue with her, but the other clubs weren't so forgiving. The start was delayed while discussions ensued.

Grace who had played Centre for the Eagles took great delight in winding Rose up. 'You must be pretty desperate to win, Rose. Shame you just missed out on the league, eh?'

'I don't know what you're talking about. Was your new player registered for the match against the Panthers by the way, I don't remember seeing the paperwork? Does anyone else?'

Gail, the umpire and Deputy Chair of the league could see where the discussion was heading.

'I'm sure we can sort this out ladies. Most of the other clubs have complained, Rose, so we need to find a compromise.'

'I'm not having this, Gail. I've been helping to run this league since...'

Lynne, the Chairwoman arrived just in time. She was less subtle than Gail. 'It's easy, Rose. You change your teams around to make it fair, or none of you will be able to play. And I don't just mean swapping around one of the Jaguar players who's already played once or twice for the Panthers this season. I'll give you a few minutes to sort it out.' She left them to it, so did Grace who sniggered and walked over to her own players, to tell them the news.

Rose blustered for a few seconds but knew she was beat. She took the sheets and called Carol and Penny over. 'You too, Chardonnay.'

'Coming, Rose.' Chardonnay tried not to look too smug. She wasn't yet sixteen but they wanted her opinion.

'Is there any chance you can get hold of Suzanne and ask her to come and play?' asked Rose.

'She's not playing for anyone at the moment sorry. She's still poorly.'

'Damn. What's wrong with her?'

Carol jumped in when she saw Chardonnay struggling to find the words. 'Never mind that, Rose. You need to change the teams now.'

'Or we'll be banned,' added Penny. 'I haven't re-arranged my schedule to be told that we can't play today.'

'Whatever I do, we're going to struggle to win this now. I'm going to make an official complaint to the league. This is discrimination...'

'Can I make a suggestion?' Chardonnay interrupted.

Rose rolled her eyes. 'What now?'

Carol smiled her encouragement.

'You pick the best, inexperienced player and put her in your team, and move one other up from the Jaguars. I would suggest Marsha and Jo.'

'Jo yes, but Marsha hasn't even played before,' said Rose.

'Whatever changes you make will weaken the team, Rose,' said Chardonnay. 'But it will show the others that our club cares about team spirit and developing all of our players, not just the first team.' Chardonnay felt like the adult talking to a stroppy teenager, and wondered why Rose couldn't see the obvious.

'Marsha has stacks of potential and she's quick to learn,' added Carol.

'You would say that, she's your new best friend.' Penny said as she looked at her nails, hoping she wouldn't have to file them any further before playing.

Carol gave Penny a warning look but decided to ignore her comment. 'As I was saying, Lynne won't budge unless we play one of the development team. It's your decision, Rose but I agree with Chardonnay.'

'Penny?'

'Whatever. As long as you don't expect me to move teams.' Penny wasn't in the best of moods. Kaitlyn was being too demanding. She was glad her daughter was playing on the other team today.

'Of course not,' said Rose.

'Let's do it then. Tell Sandy she's playing for the Jaguars today.'

'That'll work,' said Rose. 'Chardonnay, ask Sandy to come over please.' Chardonnay left as instructed. 'We'll keep Cathy but sub her on and off. You tell Sandy please, Carol while I talk to Lynne then work out the rotations with Penny.'

Sandy wouldn't be happy that's why Rose asked her to do the dirty work thought Carol, as she made her way to the group where Sandy was chatting.

'Why me, Carol and not Penny?'

'You really need to ask?' Sandy was a better player than Penny, but she wasn't as close to Rose.

'You're right. But don't expect me to be happy about it. And if we're drawn against your team, I'm not taking any prisoners.'

'I'd be the same, Sandy. But it's a fun tournament. Remember.'

They both laughed and despite Sandy's words, Carol knew she would be back to her happy self within a matter of minutes. 'Where's Marsha?'

'In the loos again.'

'Okay. When she gets back, tell her Rose wants a word.'

Having been given the news of the team change, Marsha was even more nervous. Chardonnay grabbed a few balls and called to any of the Bloomington players who were interested. 'Come on girls, let's warm up.'

As they passed the ball around and laughed and joked, she noticed Marsha starting to enjoy herself and looking less nervous. The draws completed, Lynne announced there would be a fun warm up by a new player in the Eagles team.

Marsha rushed off to the loo again – netball nerves were certainly a great laxative. She did her own hasty warm-up when she returned to the courts and didn't have time to study the opposition before Carol gave her the Goal Keeper bib.

'Don't look so worried. Rose will keep you right,' Carol gave Marsha an encouraging smile then nodded towards the opposition. 'Their new girl's playing Goal Shooter today. They've moved her up to the first team. Quite right too. And it looks like there's a new Goal Attack. I haven't seen her play before. The shooter's got a similar style of play to yours actually.' They looked at the girl as she put on her bib.

'Do your best to stick with her and remember, one eye on the ball and one on your player. And don't put your arms up to mark until you're three feet away first...' Carol looked at Marsha to ensure she'd understood. Her friend was as white as a sheet. 'Marsha?'

Marsha had stopped listening. Her heart was pounding as if to break out of her chest, the beating sound in her head almost deafening. Memories came flooding back as soon as she saw the girl who was the image of her bastard biological father. Marsha recalled the night he'd forced himself on her, her own mother's disgust, the birth, but most of all the pain when they took her baby girl away. The pain had never left but had become easier to control with each passing year.

'What is it? You look like you've seen a ghost.'

'I... I.' She couldn't possibly play against her own daughter, or could she? This might be the closest she would ever get to her if the girl didn't want to discover more about her

67

biological mother. And if she did, how could Marsha tell her she was conceived out of violence and not love?

'Sorry, Carol. Going to the loo so much must have made me feel weak. I'm okay now.'

Her colour had started to return but Carol wasn't convinced. She knew something wasn't right. 'Are you sure? You're not dizzy or anything?'

'Yeah, really. I'm fine.'

She thought Marsha was trying to convince herself more than anyone else. 'Come on then, and remember, it's only a netball match.'

'Try telling that to Rose.' They chuckled as they made their way onto court and Marsha did her best to act normal.

The majority of players were friendly and fair. Rose was an exception in that when she was on court she would do anything to win and rarely smiled or said hello to her opposite number.

Marsha knew she had to act the part. She smiled at the Goal Shooter, the girl smiled back.

'Hi, I'm Natalie. Are you okay?'

Get a grip Marsha 'Hello, Natalie,' her voice was squeaky so she coughed. 'Frog in my throat, sorry. I'm fine thanks. It's my first game so I'm a bit nervous that's all.'

'Fair enough,' said Natalie.

Rose had heard the exchange. 'Why don't you tell everyone, Marsha, so they all know you're the weak link.'

God she was such a bitch. I'm so not in the mood. 'Sorry, Rose. I didn't know it was top secret.'

Everyone who heard smiled, but the Goal Attack guffawed. 'For goodness sake, mother. It wasn't that funny,' Natalie turned to Marsha. 'It's so embarrassing being on the same team as your mother. Are you sure you're all right, you've gone a funny colour again?'

Thankfully for Marsha the umpire blew the whistle so any further conversation was halted. The players got into position.

'On my whistle, ladies.'

The opposition had the first centre pass. Following the whistle their Centre threw a quick pass to the Wing Attack. Natalie moved around the shooting circle and Marsha did her best to stay with her. The Wing Attack threw the ball straight in and Marsha jumped. The tips of two fingers just touched the ball but not enough to alter its projection. Natalie caught it just inside the circle. Marsha expected her to pass but instead, she prepared to shoot. Marsha quickly moved three feet away and leaned over, her arms covering the ball. Natalie took a sideways step and fired. Despite Marsha's best efforts the ball went in the net and the opposition gave a quick clap.

'Great shot,' said Marsha.

'Whose side are you on?' shouted Rose as she walked back into position. Marsha rolled her eyes and Natalie pulled a face at her back. They giggled silently as Natalie's mother watched. She wasn't laughing.

Unlike the league netball matches, the tournament games were two halves of ten minutes. Despite the best efforts of Natalie's team, the Panthers soon took the lead and maintained it throughout. Marsha played well but not as well as her daughter. The ball was at the Panthers end more than the Eagles and Natalie and her mother didn't have as many opportunities as the Panthers' shooters. The end result was fifteen, eleven. The teams shook hands following the final whistle.

'See you later, Marsha,' said Natalie as they shook hands. Marsha didn't trust herself to say anything and held on to Natalie's hand a second longer than she should have. Natalie gave her a strange look as she pulled back her hand.

'You're a funny one.'

She smiled at her directness. 'Sorry, I was miles away.'

'Natalie,' called her mother and she made her way to the other members of her team. Her mother gave Marsha a curious look.

'Three cheers for the Eagles and the umpires,' shouted Carol. Her team members shouted hip, hip hooray and the other team reciprocated.

The tournament progressed and as the players relaxed and chatted between matches, Marsha was silent. Carol studied her friend out of the corner of her eye. They'd played and won three and Marsha had made quite an impression. A number of players had said she was a natural netballer. Rarely was someone with so little experience that good. She was no longer nervous so her mood wasn't anything to do with the netball. They had twenty minutes until the next match so Carol made a move.

'I need to go to the shop, coming, Marsha?'

'I don't need anything thanks.'

'Come and have a walk around anyway, otherwise you'll be stiff when you get up.'

She couldn't be bothered to argue so stood up and brushed the back of her skirt where she'd been sitting on the floor. Carol waited until they were in her car.

'Do you want to talk about it?'

'What?'

'Something's not right, and I think it's to do with that youngster who plays for the Eagles.'

'I don't know what you mean.'

'Okay, Marsha. But if you ever want to talk about anything, you know you can trust me?'

'Thanks, Carol. I appreciate that.'

They drove on in silence until Carol parked the car at the supermarket. 'Life isn't simple is it?' said Marsha as she opened the door.

'It certainly isn't,' her friend replied. Carol knew she would eventually confide in her. She had an inkling about what was bothering her so decided to do a bit of digging herself. If she was right, it was little wonder that Marsha was struggling with her emotions.

They returned, played and won another match. During the next break Carol circulated and talked to other teams members. A number of them had played netball for years and knew many players outside their own teams. Lynne, the league chairwoman was talking to some of the Eagles' players. Carol moseyed over and said hi. Lynne introduced her to the new players.

'Carol this is Liz.' They said hello.

Liz explained that they'd moved there from Edinburgh a few months before. 'My husband's job brought him down South,' she said. 'Natalie's settled in well both in and out of school.'

Lynne left them to it and they carried on chatting.

'Natalie's a very good player. She has the potential to go far in netball.'

'Thanks. We're very proud of her. She didn't have a very good start in life and has come such a long way.'

'Oh really?'

Liz nodded then took a swig of her drink before answering. 'It's no secret that Natalie's adopted. Her parents died in a car crash shortly after she was born. We were told it was a

70

miracle she survived. I was desperate for a baby and she was a gift.'

'That's amazing.'

'Yeah. We've been totally open with her. Her birth parents didn't have any surviving relatives either.'

'That's very unusual,' said Carol.

'Exactly what we thought too. And the other amazing thing is just over two years after we adopted Natalie, I fell pregnant with her brother after being told it was impossible. They're nothing alike but adore each other.'

'How wonderful.' They heard a whistle. 'Lovely to chat, Liz but I'd better get a shift on, we're on next.'

'Same here, Carol. Nice to meet you. Good luck.'

The next match was relatively easy so Carol was subbed at half time so Cathy could have a run around. She watched from the sideline and looked around. Liz was watching Marsha, to the exclusion of anyone else. Nobody else appeared to be taking much notice. Her initial suspicions must have been wrong following the conversation with Liz. Unless... She decided to concentrate on the tournament and think it all through later, but something wasn't quite right and it niggled.

The Panthers won every match in their group and progressed to the playoffs. They were on a roll, winning the semi-final easily. Marsha couldn't believe that the first time she played any matches, she was going to be in the tournament final.

The other teams had gathered to watch the final. Due to the unpopularity of Rose, most teams wanted the opposition to win. Despite thinking Marsha a little weird, Natalie liked her. 'Good luck,' she called as Marsha ran onto the court to take up position.

It was a close and rough match. Both teams wanted to win and pushed as hard as they could. Drawing at half time, Rose didn't blame anyone for mistakes during the short break and the players kept their heads up during the second half. Marsha's interception gave the advantage to the Panthers and she watched as the ball was quickly passed to the other end of the court. Carol passed it to Penny whose shot was successful. The Panthers were one ahead and it was their centre pass. This time Jo, the Wing Attack passed the ball to Carol. She missed with her attempt at goal but Penny jumped up, retrieved the ball on the rebound, and

71

shot it into the net. The whistle went and the Panthers had won by two goals.

Rose pumped her fist into the air shouting yes, yes, yes. She was unbearably smug as the prizes were presented. Penny was her usual haughty self – she looked as if she'd been on a catwalk, not a netball court. She didn't appear to sweat, perspire or glow like normal women and the others wondered how she could look so pristine after running around all day.

'Well done, Marsha,' said Rose as Lynne handed out the medals. 'But there's more to come.'

'The winner of the best new player is Marsha Lawson,' said Lynne. Everyone clapped as Marsha reddened and collected her trophy.

'The player of the tournament goes to Natalie Phillips.'

Carol took a photo of Marsha and Natalie holding their awards.

Everyone clapped, then the league prizes were handed out. The Panthers accepted their prizes for second place then Lynne congratulated the Eagles. Rose wasn't so smug when Grace from the Eagles waved her trophy in front of her.

'Unlucky, Rose. There's always next year but we won't know how you do, coz we won't be here.'

Rose turned her back and silently cursed Grace. She spoke to Carol and Penny. 'Our players need to concentrate on the netball next season, and leave their personal problems at home. If we don't win the next one, that'll be my last. I've had enough.'

They nodded solemnly, neither mentioning that Rose said something similar at the end of every season.

'No training next week,' Rose reminded everyone. 'Due to half-term but we'll start for the summer league the week after.'

The hosts put the equipment away and the visitors collected all their rubbish then went their separate ways.

As soon as Carol dropped Chardonnay off, Marsha said, 'I saw you speaking to Natalie's Mum.'

Carol wasn't going to mention it but now felt she could as Marsha had raised the subject. 'Yeah. It was interesting. Natalie's adopted.'

'Really?'

Not convincing Marsha.

'Yup, really. The poor girl didn't have a very good start in life.' Carol stopped at the traffic lights and looked directly at her friend. 'Her birth parents died in a traffic accident.'

'What!'

'There were no other living relatives so the baby was adopted.'

'Is that what she told you?'

'Yes. That's exactly what Liz told me. Poor Natalie, eh?'

Carol pulled off but didn't have to look at Marsha to see she was visibly upset. As soon as she found a suitable spot to stop, she indicated and pulled over.

'It all came back to me today, I don't know how I held it together.' Marsha put her head in her hands and cried. Carol rubbed her back to comfort her, it seemed like the tears would never stop. Eventually the sobbing subsided and she took a deep breath. Her eyes looked red raw. She scrummaged in her bag for a tissue and blew her nose loudly, then looked at Carol.

'She's my daughter.'

Carol took her hand and nodded. 'I guessed.'

'Does everyone know?'

'No, Marsha. You did a good job but you haven't been yourself since seeing Natalie. Nobody else knows you well enough.'

'So only you? Good, I...'

'I think her mother, I mean Liz noticed something. You are quite alike.'

'But we look nothing like each other. Natalie's the image of her father, that's why it was such a shock.'

'You poor thing. Was he your first love?'

'As if.' She laughed bitterly. 'He was my mother's fella. She was drunk so he thought he'd have me instead.'

'You mean...?'

'I mean he raped me then my mother said I was a disgrace. Social Services took my baby away from me because I was only fourteen when she was born with nobody but an alcoholic mother in my life.'

'Oh my God, Marsha, that's so awful for you. What about your other relatives?'

'As far as I know there weren't any. My mother had a string of other boyfriends and I never felt safe after that. I met

73

Keith when I turned sixteen. My mother told him about the baby but he still agreed to take me on, even though I'd had a kid.'

'That was big of him.'

Marsha missed the sarcasm. 'Yeah it was. I left my mother's as soon as Keith suggested we move in together, then moved back into my mother's to look after her when she became ill. We married shortly after she died.' She blew her nose then continued. 'Keith's a bit old fashioned and thinks a woman's place is in the home so that's why I've never worked until now, and he doesn't like it.' She started to cry again and Carol enveloped her in a hug.

She wiped her eyes when she stopped and looked at her friend. 'I feel like my whole life is imploding. We've lost our house, I'm losing my husband and I find out today that my daughter thinks I'm dead. I might as well be.'

'Don't you ever say that,' Carol unhugged her and held both of her arms. 'You are one of the best people I have ever met. You've changed your mother-in-law's attitude and she now enjoys life for the first time in years. You've got a steady job and people who care about you. I know today has been a complete shock, Marsha, but it's not the end of the world.'

'It feels like it,' Marsha muttered.

'It's bound to. But you can go to the authorities and ask them to contact Natalie on your behalf. I don't believe that Social Services would have told Liz and her husband that Natalie's birth parents had died.'

'So you think she made it up?'

'It seems likely to me, yes, but I don't know that for a fact. Maybe she doesn't want Natalie looking for her birth parents. Don't hold it against her. Adoptive parents can feel insecure too you know. It doesn't have to be the end of the world.'

Marsha gave a weak smile. 'On the day I find my daughter, I discover that she thinks I'm dead. It seems like my world has ended.'

'I get that. But it hasn't. Shall we get you home?'

'Thanks. I've got a lot to think about.'

They sat in silence for the rest of the journey, Carol sneaking the occasional look at her to check she was okay. Both saw the blue light flashing as they turned the corner onto Marsha's street.

74

'Wonder what's happened there?' asked Carol. Then she realised the ambulance was parked outside Ann's house.

'Stop the car,' shouted Marsha. 'Now, Carol. Quick.'

Carol hit the brakes and Marsha flung open the passenger door. She ran towards Ann's house with Carol close on her heels.

Chapter 10

When Sandy returned from the tournament she wondered if she'd entered the wrong house. She listened to the romantic ballad and entered the kitchen-diner. The small table was set with cutlery and napkins. Leon was standing next to the fridge holding an open bottle of beer and grinning

'This looks lovely, what's happened?'

He laughed. 'Nothing. I thought you wouldn't want to cook after playing netball all day.'

Oh shit. 'Have you cooked, Leon?'

'Don't be stupid, Sandy,' the smile disappeared from his face. 'I am your husband, I do not need to cook.' He opened the oven and grinned again. 'But we have Chinese.'

'Oh, what a lovely surprise.'

Leon put the hot plate on the work surface so his wife could hug him. He lifted her and swung her around.

'See. I can be a modern man.'

'Of course you can.' Sandy knew something was up but daren't mention it. But she was determined to find out what was going on. She wondered if it was to do with the day before when he told her he had to work late in the stores due to an audit. He hadn't been there when she'd phoned and the Private soldier he worked with knew nothing about the audit. Leon had said the man was an idiot and that was the end of it. She had brushed it off but now smelled a rat. He had never helped in the kitchen in over eight years of marriage, considering it woman's work. Sandy was surprised he knew how to switch on the oven.

'Sit down. Glass of wine?'

The rat got bigger.

They had a lovely meal and evening. Leon watched some football while she tidied up the kitchen.

'I know it's hard for you without the kids, but it won't be much longer.' His comment came from nowhere and it totally threw her. He must miss their babies too.

'It is and it's going to take a while to get the money together. But I'm putting away as much as I can so we can get them over here and give them the life they deserve,' said Sandy and her husband kissed the top of her head.

'In bed later they made love like newlyweds. The light off, Sandy felt safer speaking into the darkness.

'Is everything all right, Leon?'

His snoring told her she wasn't getting an answer that night.

*****

A trolley was being wheeled out of the house as Marsha's feet hit the pavement outside. Ann came running out of the house behind it. She pulled at the arm of the paramedic.

'No, no, no. Not my baby. Please try again, please.'

'I'm sorry love,' the paramedic shook his head.

Marsha was rooted to the spot as the events unfolding in front of her played in slow motion, while she tried to take it all in. The paramedics wheeled the trolley to the back of the ambulance as her mother-in-law kept hold of the arm of one of them. He stopped and tried to console her. When he saw Marsha his eyes beseeched her for help.

She looked at the trolley with the sheet covering the entirety of the body; then it clicked. When Marsha realised it was her husband's body her initial reaction was one of relief. Then she put her hands on her head exactly as she did when she saw a mouse or creepy crawly and was consumed with fear. A spurt of guilt came next followed by a sense of loss. She must have loved him even though he was a total bastard.

'Ann?'

Ann noticed her daughter-in-law for the first time. 'Marsha, love. It's Keith. He's, he's…'

A paramedic came to her side and took her arm. She sat on the wall as he explained. 'Are you Keith's wife?'

She could barely nod.

'I'm so sorry. He had a massive heart attack. He was already dead by the time we arrived. We did try to bring him back but…'

'Try again. Please try one more time. Pleeeeeeeese.' The last word was a scream as Ann broke down completely. Marsha hurried to her side and hugged her. Both women were shaking.

As she held Ann, she addressed a paramedic as they loaded the trolley into the ambulance. 'I want to see him.'

'Of course, love.'

'Can you take my mother-in-law inside?'

As one took Ann into the house, the other led Marsha onto the back of the ambulance. He pulled the sheet from Keith's face. She took a step back. The colour had already drained from

77

his face and his lips were blue. To Marsha, he looked like a wax replica of her husband. It was as if Keith had already left. She wondered which way he had gone but quickly wiped that thought from her mind. She touched his cheek; there was no warmth.

'Thank you for taking me on,' she said. 'It would have been so much better if you were kinder.' She reached down and kissed his cheek. 'Goodbye, Keith.'

'Thank you,' she said to the paramedic as she stood up. She put her hand to her mouth and bit on the fleshy part of her finger, trying to hold it together until at least inside the house. A small crowd had formed on the street and they watched as she made her way in from the ambulance.

Carol was already in the house, sitting next to Ann on the settee and holding her while she sobbed her heart out.

'Oh, Marsha,' said Ann. 'What are we going to do?'

Carol extricated herself and Marsha took her place. The two women held each other and sobbed. Carol felt like an intruder. She knew it wouldn't help but went to the kitchen to make a brew. By the time she returned with three mugs on a tray with some sugar in a bowl and the bottle of milk, the women had quieted. They were sitting next to each other staring into space, consumed by their own thoughts.

'Here's some tea.' She put the tray down on the coffee table in front of the settee.

'Thanks,' said Marsha.

Carol took a seat and they drank in silence. She put her mug on the tray when it was half empty. 'If you need anything?'

Marsha nodded towards the kitchen and Carol followed her. 'I don't know what to do. I've never had to...' she sobbed and tried again. 'The paramedic said I'd get a death certificate once a doctor certified him dead at the hospital. I'll have to think about a funeral. I don't know how I'm going to pay for it, we don't have any money.'

'I had insurance,' said Ann. Neither had noticed her presence. 'Come and sit down, Marsha. I need to talk to you.'

'I'll go,' said Carol. 'But I'll come round tomorrow to help with anything you need.'

After saying goodbye Carol saw herself out.

On the settee Ann took both of Marsha's hands in hers. 'You know Keith's father died when he was five years old. He had a heart condition and I discovered that his paternal

78

grandfather had also died of a heart attack when young. I've tried to talk to Keith about it a number of times since he's grown up. You know how he loves his football? Well he always said that kept him fit and there was nothing wrong with his heart.'

'But why didn't he tell me?' asked Marsha.

'I don't know. He made me promise not to say anything and must have believed that nothing would happen to him. But he was wrong.' The last was said on a sob and Marsha held Ann as she cried. It seemed they stayed like that for a long time. Marsha's eyes were dry as she thought about her life with her husband. She'd seen little of him since they'd lived with his mother. When he did make an appearance he was unkind and the atmosphere was much better when he was out of the house. She would still miss him, if only out of habit. Feeling a sense of guilt as she held Ann, Marsha tried to wipe the last thought from her head. Ann had lost a son. There was no pain to compare with losing a child, no matter their age. She knew that from her own bitter experience but at least Natalie was alive and well. She felt guilty again as she thought of her wonderful daughter, when her dead husband should have been the only one on her mind.

*****

The days leading up to the funeral felt unreal. It was as if everything was in a haze and Marsha was looking at herself from the outside, wondering what this strange woman would do next. Keith's death had shocked them both and Ann took to her bed most days. When she did get up, she sat staring at the television as she had when they first moved in and only spoke when she had to. Marsha was on autopilot and would have broken down herself without the support and friendship of Carol. Ann and Marsha were in no fit state to make all the funeral arrangements, but with Carol's help, it was less overwhelming.

It rained before, during and after the funeral. Ann was inconsolable and Marsha was numb. Keith's new and old colleagues were there, along with his mates from football. One of them gave an emotional tribute and Marsha didn't recognise the funny and thoughtful man he was describing, not even from the early days of their marriage. They drank a toast to Keith in their football pub where Marsha and Carol had arranged a small buffet paid for by Ann.

In bed that night she wondered what she would do with the rest of her life, but decided to take it one day at a time.

79

Marsha wanted to keep busy and was ready to return to work a few days after Keith's funeral. Carol advised her to take a few weeks off. 'Firstly, it will be easier for Ann if you're at home. The other thing is,' she hesitated.

'What is it, Carol?'

'You know how people talk, just give it time.'

'You mean somebody might notice that I'm not broken hearted?'

'I didn't mean that?'

Marsha gave her a look.

'All right then, I did.'

'Look, Carol. You know how Keith treated me,' she didn't wait for an answer. 'I think I still loved him in my own way but I didn't like him. Even his mother didn't like him,' she whispered the last as if Ann might walk in at any minute. 'I've spent years pretending and hoping that my life might get better, and now it has I can't pretend anymore.'

'Fair enough.'

It was as if the floodgates had opened and Marsha had so much to get out of her system. 'Since Keith started working at the camp we've seen each other less and less. The only time he wanted sex was a quick fumble and only after he'd been drinking. I was relieved he stopped trying to force himself on me like he used to. We both wanted kids and I was willing to give it a try but Keith wouldn't see a doctor, refusing to have his masculinity questioned as he saw it. It got worse from there and I'm convinced he was seeing someone else. I already thought about leaving him and started to squirrel away a few quid every week.'

'I knew you weren't happy, but you kept the rest of this to yourself?'

'Believe it or not Ann and I have become good friends. She told me she loved her son but didn't like him and started supporting me when he was abusive.'

Carol raised her eyebrows.

'He always had a sharp tongue but hasn't laid a finger on me since we've lived with his mother.'

'I see.'

'I'm still getting my head around it all but when I woke up the day after the funeral it was as if a massive weight had been lifted and I didn't feel guilty any more. I felt relieved, Carol, and if that makes me a bad person, so be it.'

'Oh, Marsha. You wouldn't know how to be a bad person,' she leaned over and gave her arm a squeeze. 'So what are you going to do?'

'I'll take your advice and look after Ann, but I want to return to work and netball too. The only other thing I know for definite at the moment, is that I'm going to approach the authorities when Natalie's eighteen and ask them to let her know about me.'

Carol looked at her friend with pride and affection. Marsha had come such a long way in the short time they'd known each other. She silently wished her a future filled with love, luck and lots of fun. All of which had been sadly missing up until now.

*****

Marsha had been feeling better, until she returned to work. Within half an hour she wanted to go home; her colleagues either approached her and quickly told her how sorry they were, or avoided her like the plague. Death seemed awkward for everyone, except the dearly - or not so dearly in this case - departed. Those that really knew her were the exception.

Carol visited the diner within half an hour of Marsha's arrival.

'Will you think I'm stupid if I ask how you are?'

'No,' she said and laughed. Other members of staff looked her way as if she had two heads. 'I feel like I'm on reality TV. Everything I do is being analysed.'

'Don't worry they'll soon get over it. You knew the first day was going to be the worst. Look, here's Gary.'

Gary had been a regular customer since Marsha's first day and she enjoyed the banter between them. Her face lit up as he walked toward her.

'I'm so sorry for your loss, love.'

Something tore at her heart as she saw the genuine concern on his face and Marsha burst into tears. He held her and Carol didn't need to look around, knowing the others had stopped working and were staring at the couple. This would be all over the camp by lunchtime. She coughed discreetly, but they were in their own world. Marsha broke the embrace. She rubbed at her eyes and tried to laugh it off.

'Sorry about that. It happens when I least expect it.' She took a tissue out of her overall pocket and wiped her nose just in

81

time. 'My God, I'm a wreck. I'll get you a coffee, Gary when I've sorted myself out. Give me a few minutes please.'

Before he could answer she'd hurried to the ladies. Carol quickly followed.

Marsha was rinsing her face in cold water. 'I don't know what's come over me. I held it together until...'

'It's early days, Marsha, give it time.'

'You're right of course,' she blew her nose loudly and they both laughed. 'As always.'

'I'd best get back to work.'

As she went to open the door Carol put her hand on her arm. 'Marsha,' her friend turned. 'You know people will talk?'

'I don't care, Carol. I've spent years being miserable and worrying that I'm not good enough. Now I realise it was Keith's way of controlling me. Life is short and if people want to think the worst of me, so be it. But there's nothing going on anyway. My emotions are all over the place and it's far too soon.'

'Perhaps you need to explain that to Gary.'

'Oh God. This is all I need. Okay, I'll have a word. But not today. I just want to get through my first day back and hopefully it'll get easier.'

'I need to go into town after work. I'll pick you up after you finish and give you a lift home if you like?'

Marsha knew she was probably lying about going to town but appreciated the offer. 'That would be great, ta.'

They said their goodbyes and both returned to work.

Chapter 11

Sandy and Leon had just finished eating. 'I'm on duty tomorrow night,' he called from the living room as she was clearing up the dishes in the kitchen.

'But you were on duty last weekend, what's going on?' This would be the third time this month, which was unusual.

'I'm doing a favour for one of the boys so he can take his wife out on their anniversary. He'll help me out when I need it.'

'Who's that then?'

'Nobody you know, Sandy.'

'Okay.' He was obviously lying but she had no idea why.

'I'm going for a bath.' End of conversation as Leon left the room.

Sandy waited until she heard the bathroom door close then rummaged through his combat jacket pocket. She retrieved his phone and put it on the coffee table. She went to the bottom of the stairs and listened. Hearing nothing she knew he was relaxing in the bath. She quickly took the phone into the kitchen. Having watched him unlock his phone when he'd been drinking she now keyed the code she'd memorised. There were no suspicious messages or texts so she checked out his apps. He had one called *mobile ticket,* which she opened. She was surprised to discover a pre-booked ticket for the following afternoon, returning the Saturday morning. He hadn't deleted his previous journey details and Sandy found three others. She switched the phone off, returned it to his jacket pocket and put it away. So he was seeing someone else. She made herself a cup of tea while deciding what to do.

*****

Kaitlyn and Evie returned from their holiday in the sun.

'I'll see you on Facebook and Instagram. Let's do something together this Christmas,' said Kaitlyn.

Evie gave her friend a hug, she would miss her but it was better to say nothing rather than lie. The money from Kat's father meant she could leave university debt free. Breaking her ties with Kat was part of the deal. On balance it was a small price to pay.

'You take care of yourself, and get a proper job.'

Kaitlyn nodded, knowing she had no choice in the matter if she wanted her father's emotional and financial support. They had one final hug then headed for trains to different parts of the country. Kaitlyn was certainly bronzed from her holiday but not relaxed, having had plenty of time to reflect on the past and plan for the future. Before she did that, she wanted to know if there was any truth in what her father had said about her mother. She recalled the conversation in the hotel room when she thought her father had lied about her mother to justify his own behaviour. For some reason it wouldn't go away. As it replayed over and over in her mind, she knew she had to get to the bottom of it. Her father had told her not to say anything so she had to come up with a less direct approach.

Although genuinely pleased to see her, she detected something in her mother's tone that she wasn't sure of.

'Kaitlyn, darling, you look like a bronzed goddess. Did you have fun?'

'It was great, Mummy. I'm going to miss Evie. How about we have that girlie night in and I can tell you all about it.'

'Wonderful idea, darling. Tomorrow night?' Penny played with her phone while waiting for her daughter's answer.

'I'm out tomorrow. Let's do it tonight.'

'Oh, Kaitlyn I can't darling. I've arranged to meet Felicity later today. We're going shopping and to the theatre, then overnighting in London.'

'That sounds great, Mummy. I'll come with you.'

'No.' Seeing the look of surprise on her daughter's face she elaborated. 'What I mean, darling is that Felicity has some problems. She won't discuss them if you're there, so I'm sorry. And anyway, you'd soon be bored with our company.'

'But...'

'No buts, darling. I'm sorry. How about Sunday?'

'Sunday it is then.'

While Kaitlyn suspected her mother was up to something, Penny was determined to put more effort into her appearance, so she wouldn't be completely upstaged by her gorgeous daughter whenever they were together.

*****

Kaitlyn unpacked quickly and returned downstairs. Maureen was in the kitchen. She asked her to make a quick lunch.

'Where's Mum?'

'In her bathroom. She's pampering herself and says she doesn't want to be disturbed.'

'Thanks, Maureen. What time is Eddie picking her up?'

84

The Housekeeper looked at her watch. 'He'll be here any time now. I usually give him lunch before he takes your mother to catch the two o'clock train.'

'Is it a regular thing then?'

'She goes up to London quite often, yes. You know your mother enjoys the theatre. Depending on her plans she either stays overnight or comes home late Friday night. When Eddie wants the weekend off she's quite happy to get a taxi back from the station.'

'I see. So how often is...'

'Why don't you ask your mother, Kaitlyn?' said Maureen.

'I didn't want to disturb her. Anyway, thanks for lunch. I'm off out. Tell Mum I'll see her tomorrow please.'

'Will do. Do you want Eddie to give you a lift somewhere?'

'No, I'm fine thanks.' She didn't want anyone else to know where she was going.

At Waterloo station Kaitlyn waited for the 2 o'clock train from Harrington Water. It was due in at platform sixteen and she'd need her wits about her at the busy station to follow her mother. On the upside, her mother was far less likely to spot her amongst so many people, but Kaitlyn had put her hair up and wore jeans, a bomber jacket and baseball cap. The good thing about London was you could wear anything and not look out of place.

It was obvious her mother was heading for the underground and Kaitlyn followed. They both had Oyster cards so she tried to keep her distance but also remain close enough so she wouldn't lose sight of her. As her mother entered the platform, she hung back until she heard the train approaching. Seeing her mother's blonde head disappear into a carriage, she hopped onto the carriage next door, just before the door closed. She alighted at Charing Cross and followed again at a discreet distance. It was no surprise when her mother entered the Savoy. She watched her check-in and saw the direction she headed. Kaitlyn removed her baseball cap and jacket and put them in the large bag she'd brought with her. She went to the ladies where she tidied her hair and applied some lipstick before entering the hotel's foyer. Taking a comfortable seat at a booth in the cafe bar where she could see the lift her mother used, she ordered a coffee and took her laptop out of her bag. She watched people come and go but didn't recognise anyone. Unless she'd missed her, her mother's friend Felicity hadn't arrived. Half an hour later, she was surprised to see a face she recognised. It was Sandy, one of the Fijian netball players. Sandy was watching the lift as a man entered it. Then she looked around as if wondering what to do. As one of the staff approached her, Kaitlyn made her presence known.

'Hey, Sandy.'

Sandy looked around trying to find the owner of the voice. Kaitlyn stood up and waved and was surprised that Sandy wasn't smiling at her. Although she hadn't seen her for a few months, they were netball mates and knew each other well enough. She beckoned her over and Sandy reluctantly made her way to the booth.

'Fancy seeing you here. How are you?' she asked.

'Kaitlyn. I didn't expect.... You haven't seen me, okay. If anyone asks you definitely haven't seen me.' Sandy was looking around all the while.

'I see. Don't worry I won't say a word to anyone. What's wrong?'

Sandy burst into tears, which drew the attention of other guests.

'I need to leave.'

She was distraught and Kaitlyn didn't want to leave her in that condition. She was also intrigued. 'Okay, I'll come with you,' she quickly paid her bill. 'Let's find somewhere where we can talk.'

They walked to the end of the road and down a side street. It wasn't long before they found a cosy little cafe bar.

'Tea, coffee or something stronger?' asked Kaitlyn.

'I think I'd better have a glass of wine.' Sandy rubbed at her eyes. 'Sorry about making an idiot of myself back there. It's just...'

'It's okay. What's happened?'

'It's my husband Leon. I think he's cheating on me.'

'What makes you say that?'

Sandy explained about looking at the tickets on his phone, Leon lying about being on duty, and how she'd discovered he wasn't in work one day when he should have been.

'But there's no way on earth he could afford a room in the Savoy.'

86

Kaitlyn put two and two together and came up with a horrendous mental picture.

'Are you okay, Kaitlyn?'

'Yes, sorry, I'm fine. What are you going to do?'

'I'm not sure. I need a bit of time. That's why you can't tell anyone you've seen me. Promise?'

'I promise,' she said. 'Look, if you need to talk or a shoulder to cry on, I'm about for the next few weeks. Here's my number.' She wrote it down and Sandy took the piece of paper.

'If we split up I'll have to return to Fiji. At least I'd get to see my kids sooner than expected.' She gave a sad laugh. 'But I love him and I thought he loved me. I just don't understand it, Leon's a good guy.'

Kaitlyn let her vent for a bit. She knew that some of the Fijian families took their children home for their parents to look after; it must have been hard for Sandy. Now that she'd stopped crying, Kaitlyn didn't think it was the right time to ask her about her kids in case it started her off again.

'Thanks for listening. What brings you to London?'

'I'm meeting some friends. Actually, I'm late already so I'd better get moving. That's if you're okay?'

'I'm better than I was thanks. I'll make my way home and decide when I'm going to speak to Leon. Are you playing in the tournament? Maybe see you there?'

'Yeah. See you there.'

She paid for the drinks and Sandy left her to it. As soon as she was out of sight she phoned her mother.

'Kaitlyn?'

'Hi, Mummy. I'm after a favour.'

'Make it quick we're about to go into the underground.'

'I forgot to ask you earlier. Can you pick me up a charm for my Pandora bracelet if I message you the picture?' There wasn't a Pandora shop in Harrington Water.

'Of course, darling. Send me the piccy and I'll bring it home with me.'

'Thanks, Mummy. Oh and what show are you going to see?'

'The Jersey Boys. Must rush. Bye, darling. Love you.'

'You too. Bye, Mummy.'

She made her way to the Piccadilly Theatre and hung around until thirty minutes after the show had started. She'd watched carefully and her mother hadn't put in an appearance. Now believing her father had told the truth, Kaitlyn recalled his words. He'd said that her mother liked exotic men. Was it coincidence that Sandy's husband was in the same place as her mother on the same day?

*****

Ann was coming to terms with Keith's death, and slowly coming out of the depression it had caused. She started to spend less time in front of the TV and engaged Marsha in conversation. The most promising action was less than three months after Keith's death when Marsha woke up to a noise. She got up to investigate; it was coming from the third bedroom. Poking her head around the door she took in the scene. Ann was surrounded by a number of black dustbin bags that were already full. Space could be seen on the floor and furniture for the first time since Marsha had lived there, and she thought, probably the first time in years. Ann was crying to herself and Marsha heard her whisper over and over. 'It's only stuff.'

'Ann?'

'Oh, Marsha,' she threw her half-empty bag on the floor. 'I know it's only things but it's so hard. I can't hold on to people so I only have my belongings.' Marsha stepped into the room and gave her mother-in-law a hug. Neither felt awkward and Marsha put aside the regret that they could have had this friendship years before.

'You don't have to do this, Ann. Not if it upsets you.'

'I know, but I need to talk to you.' There was now space on the bed so they sat down. 'My counsellor says this will help and,' she smiled. 'I've met someone. His name's Colin and I wondered if you'd help me cook him dinner one night and then... um then...'

'Then disappear?'

Ann laughed. 'Yes please.'

'That's great news, Ann.'

'He's so kind and it's like a new chapter for me. I feel ready to get rid of some of this...' she waved her hand around the room. 'Get rid of this crap from my life. It's been hindering me for too long.'

It wasn't only the material baggage Ann was referring to.

*****

The summer break was over and Kaitlyn had settled into her new university and was working in a local bar during down time. She knew her father had people watching her but didn't have a clue about who or when. It was frustrating but she had to behave. There was nobody she clicked with and despite her best efforts she'd been unable to contact Evie. It had upset her at first, but now she was annoyed with her friend so tried not to think about it. Instead, she knuckled down and worked hard both in and out of class, but still needed something else to do during her down time. Instead of being bored she focused on discovering more about her mother's movements, which had proved relatively easy. Any time off during her course was on a Friday so the students could travel home if they wished. Felicity was always her mother's excuse so when she phoned to say she'd be home that weekend, she knew what her mother was up to if it involved Felicity. Maureen had confirmed her mother was a creature of habit and whilst she was discreet during the time at the hotel, she always caught the same train there and back. Kaitlyn had seen the big Fijian arrive always within an hour of her mother's arrival and she was certain they were lovers. Her mother was a money-grabbing slapper and her father a hypocrite, and she wasn't even permitted to have the lifestyle afforded by her father's money. The injustices of life simmered as the weeks passed and she was determined to get back at them both, without losing her inheritance.

Then she received the email from Sandy that proved her suspicions correct.

*****

Penny's good mood disappeared when she saw her husband's Range Rover outside the mansion. *Shit, Paul must be home early.* She wasn't in the mood for playing the game but knew she had to. Her lifestyle was easier to maintain with Paul providing the funds and respectability she needed. She parked the car and centred herself. The car's inside lights were off as Penny lifted her hand above her head, closed her eyes and pulled her hand down in front of her face to her abdomen. She plastered on a smile, left the car and approached the house. She was humming a tune by the time she opened the front door and keyed in the security code in the box next to the door.

89

'Paul, darling. What a wonderful surprise,' she quickly hung her jacket in the hallway cupboard and made her way to the lounge where the lights were on. 'Oh, I've missed you so much.'

Paul put down his whisky tumbler and got to his feet. His wife ran into his arms and they hugged passionately. He didn't understand how she could be so enthusiastic when he knew she was fucking any young stag she could get her hands on. Despite this knowledge, she still excited him.

'Penny,' he breathed in her unique scent. 'It's good to be home.' He meant it, but not for the reasons she thought.

'Let's go to bed,' said Penny.

He led the way.

He knew her mind was elsewhere as he satisfied himself with her body. It didn't make any difference, he still enjoyed it. After they'd finished Paul grunted and rolled off his wife. She got up straight away and put on her negligee.

'Whisky, darling?'

'I think champagne is in order. I have news.'

'I'll get it. Won't be a tick.'

As Penny made her way to the kitchen, Paul left their bed and put on his dressing gown. He went to the bathroom and dried off the rose he'd placed in a pint pot earlier. He put it on the bed and extracted the envelope from his briefcase and placed it on the bed, next to the rose. He admired his handiwork as Penny entered the bedroom with the champagne and glasses.

'Ooh, that looks interesting.' The envelope had Penny's name on the front in embossed lettering. 'What have you got for me?' She picked up the envelope and ran a finger over her name. Turning it over she started to open it.

She's not interested in the rose because it doesn't have any monetary value, thought Paul as he took the envelope from her.

'All will become clear, Penny. Here,' he picked up the champagne and popped the cork. 'Pour the drinks and I'll explain.'

Intrigued, Penny did as told.

'Do you know what our daughter used to do to earn money?' said Paul. 'Before she moved universities?'

Penny wondered what that had to do with the envelope. She could see he was being serious so decided to play along.

90

'Of course, darling. She worked in a bar. Like she does now.'

'I wish that were true. Our daughter was a high-class hooker.'

Penny laughed. 'Don't be ridiculous, darling. Why would you say such a thing? And why are we drinking champagne when you're obviously not in the mood for celebrating your return.'

'Firstly, darling,' Paul emphasised the word, 'I had Brian check out Kaitlyn's job and he came back to me with the news. I've had it out with her and that's why she moved university. Now I have someone watching her, to keep her on the straight and narrow.'

'Oh that's awful. But if you'd given her a decent allowance she wouldn't have had to steep so low.'

Most women would have been mortified to discover their daughter was a prostitute. Not Penny, the money was her main concern. Paul wasn't surprised.

'And if her mother didn't act like a cheap whore, perhaps Kaitlyn would have chosen a different path.' Paul calmly placed his glass down on his bedside cabinet. Penny noticed the veins raised in his neck and knew he was on the verge of losing it.

'I don't know what you're talking about, Paul. You're obviously still upset about Kaitlyn. It must have been simmering all this time. I'll speak to her, darling and everything will be fine again with you two. I know you adore each other. Don't worry, but please don't take it out on me.'

'But you do know what I'm talking about, Penny darling,' he leaned over and produced an A4 size brown envelope out of which he took a photograph. 'Recognise this man?'

Penny paled but was still in denial. 'No idea, Paul. Who is he?'

'His name is Sayid and he now lives in Scotland. That's why he didn't answer any of your calls Penny, darling.' He took another photograph out of the envelope. 'Does he look familiar, Penny? The husband of one of your netball team. That's low even by your standards.'

She knew there was no point denying it further. 'But, Paul, darling. I didn't know. You have to believe me.'

He ignored her and took the last two photographs out of the envelope and laid them on the bed. They showed Penny

91

sleeping, wearing nothing but a small satisfied smile. Tears were streaming down her face. She would kill that bastard Leon, deceiving her after all she'd given him.

'Now you can open the envelope.'

'But... I...'

'Open the envelope. Now.'

She did as instructed. Inside was an official looking document. Penny scanned it quickly, shaking her head as she tried to make sense of it.

'You can't do this to me. We've been married over twenty years and if you divorce me I'm entitled to half of everything. I've held this family together.'

'Shut up, Penny and listen. If you don't agree to this I'll make sure everyone knows about your affairs and...'

'You do that, Paul and I'll tell everyone what your precious daughter's been up to. You'll be the laughing stock at your club.'

She didn't see the slap coming and put her hand up to her stinging face. 'You hit me! How could you?' Penny screamed. He had never laid a finger on her during their life together.

Paul instantly regretted the slap. He wasn't the sort of man to hit women, no matter what the provocation. And now he'd hit his wife as well as his daughter. He took a moment to calm down and spoke as if in his boardroom. 'You'd shame your own daughter for the sake of your lifestyle? You really are one nasty piece of work.'

'And you're a fucking hypocrite, Paul. Do you think I don't know about you carrying on with any cheap piece of meat when you go away?' Seeing his surprise she continued. 'How do you think that made me feel, eh?'

'I wouldn't need to if you had showed the slightest bit of interest in anything other than money.' Paul started to dress. 'We will divorce and my lawyers will be in touch.'

'Remember what I said, Paul. I won't go down without a fight.'

He slammed every door on the way out. Penny thought she'd be happy but she didn't want a divorce. The revelation about Kaitlyn's last job was at the back of her mind, as she wondered if she could use it to stop Paul divorcing her.

Paul called Eddie first. He'd had too much alcohol to drive and even if he hadn't, he needed time to think. The driver got the message when his boss closed the door between the front and back of the limo. Mr Mason didn't want to talk, and that was fine by him. He called the hotel to book rooms and Brian met him there a few minutes after Eddie dropped him off.

'She's willing to sacrifice her daughter's good name in order to get more money. Can you fucking believe it?'

Unfortunately Brian could and he told his friend as much. 'At the risk of upsetting you further, I told you what she was like years ago. You chose to ignore my advice.'

Paul's face was like thunder. Brian tensed, waiting for the onslaught. The anger evaporated as quickly as it appeared and Paul started to cry. Brian had never seen him so upset.

'For fuck's sake,' said Paul, embarrassed. 'I still love the bitch after all she's done to me.'

Brian put his arm around him and Paul grabbed him in a full man hug, crying into his shoulder. This was another first and although feeling awkward, Brian held him until the sobbing subsided.

'Whisky?' he asked as they broke apart and Paul coughed. Neither made eye contact as Brian took the small bottles out of the mini-bar. 'I'd better ring room service,' he said. Both laughed and the earlier tears and hug were locked away in a mental folder under the heading *never to be mentioned again*.

Paul took a quick shower and sorted himself out while Brian ordered food and drink. 'What do you want to do, Paul?'

'I can't go on like this. I'm going to divorce the bitch and her settlement will be as small as I can get away with.'

'You sure about this?'

He said he was. 'But I need to speak to Kaitlyn so she knows what her mother is really like. I'm going to cut her some slack and give her a decent allowance. I don't want to lose my daughter as well as my wife. I'll phone her shortly to tell her I'm going to see her tomorrow. She's coming home next weekend for her netball so needs to know what's going on before then.'

'Kaitlyn's definitely learnt her lesson and is knuckling down so I think that's a good decision. But what about Penny? Do you want to risk her dragging it through the courts?'

Paul was aware that everyone would know their family business if that happened, but his need for revenge was great. 'I'll speak to Kaitlyn and let you know early next week. Now let's enjoy this dinner and watch a kick-ass movie to take my mind off all of this crap.'

*****

Kaitlyn was sitting at a quiet corner table in the upmarket restaurant, waiting for her father to arrive. Despite their falling out he had changed his mind and she was to receive a decent monthly allowance. She'd heard the love in his voice when he'd spoken to her the previous night and that, along with the news about the allowance, had softened her attitude towards him. She was looking forward to seeing him. They hugged when he arrived and she told him her news as they ordered drinks and scanned the menu. As soon as the waiter left with their order, Paul cut to the chase.

'So Mummy said she'd tell all of your friends about me, my,..'

'Let's call it your mistake, Kaitlyn.'

'Fine, Daddy. Mummy would be willing to let everyone know *my mistake* just to get more money from you?'

'That's what she said to me, yes.'

Kaitlyn thought for a moment, trying to get her head around her father's revelation. 'Seriously, Daddy? You're not kidding?'

'No, darling. Sorry but it's the truth.'

Watching as his daughter struggled with her emotions, he gave her a few moments.

'Kaitlyn?'

She wasn't doing a very good job of holding it together, so he moved to her side and took her in his arms. She'd made a mistake but was still his baby girl. The other diners tried to avert their eyes.

'We're a proper fucked up family aren't we, Daddy?' she whispered.

'Kaitlyn! You weren't brought up to use that sort of language.' *She wasn't brought up to be a prostitute either, but he tried to wipe that thought from his mind.*

'Sorry, Daddy. Despite everything I really thought Mummy loved me, in her own way. But she wouldn't do this to me if she did. Is there anything you can do to stop her?'

'I'm sorry, Kaitlyn. I wish I hadn't said anything to her. But your mother has given me a figure for her silence. I'm not

94

happy about it but am willing to pay if it means your mistake is kept secret.'

'You'd do that for me, after everything that's happened?'

'Yes, darling, of course I would. I'm not happy about what she's asked for but you seem to have settled in well here and have knuckled down. I don't want to ruin your future.'

'Oh, Daddy.' Kaitlyn flung her arms around his neck and hugged him as hard as she could. Although they were a messed up family, she knew she was forgiven and it was the best feeling in the world. Now she knew the truth about her mother, she felt sympathy for her father and his predicament. She figured it was her mother's fault and she shouldn't be able to walk away scot-free.

'When I'm back for netball next weekend I'm not going to stay at home. I want to surprise Mummy so can you tell her I'm too upset to come home or something?'

'Of course. What do you have in mind?'

Kaitlyn outlined her plan and Paul laughed without humour. His daughter would go far.

'I'm going to make her suffer before I agree to her settlement,' he saw the fear in his daughter's eyes. 'Don't worry. She won't say anything about you as long as she knows there's a chance of a decent amount of money. Will you be okay until the weekend or do you want me to hang around for a few days?'

She realised he was over-compensating because she now knew her mother's real feelings, but Kaitlyn enjoyed being cherished by her father. If there was one good thing to come out of this mess, it was that they had healed their wounds and could get back to being close.

'I'll be fine, Daddy if you can stay for a few hours after dinner?'

'Of course, Princess.' He hadn't called her that for years, and she didn't object.

95

Chapter 12

'Post,' Sam shouted.

As Carol ran down the stairs, he was looking through it. 'Mostly junk,' he said discarding the annoying flyers and paperwork offering them the world.

'Has my parcel arrived?' She was waiting for some new netball kit.

'No, love sorry, but what's this?' He pulled out a cream envelope addressed to Carol. Unable to make out the postmark, he passed it his wife.

She recognised the handwriting as soon as she read it and Sam saw her reaction straight away.

'Are you all right, love?'

'It's from Callum.' Her statement spoke volumes and many painful memories from years before invaded her thoughts. Life as Mark had been a living hell for Carol and her ex wife Gaynor had been disgusted when Carol finally told her that he wanted to be a woman. Gaynor had made it her mission to turn the boys against her soon to be ex husband. Callum had been fifteen and Brent thirteen. They were both upset and confused by their father's confession. Callum had lashed out and said they didn't want to see Carol again if she insisted on wearing dresses and makeup. Carol knew that if she had been forced to remain living as Mark and not admit who she really was, it would have killed her. The support worker told her that after the shock wore off, children often wanted to be back in touch with their parent, but warned that wasn't always the case. Some couldn't accept the situation, and such a momentous change of life sometimes made family members feel totally alienated with no desire to be in touch with their former loved ones, ever again. Although it had been the hardest decision of her life, she'd felt she had no choice. That had been five years before and every day she thought of her boys, knowing she'd abandoned them when they'd needed their father the most.

Carol read the letter, savouring every word.

'What's the news?'

She'd almost forgotten Sam was there. He'd made his views clear on the situation years before and it wasn't something they discussed further. The longer there was no contact, the less they expected to hear from her boys.

'Can we do this later, Sam. I need to get to the tournament.'

'Some things are more important than bloody netball.' He knew she was playing for time but wasn't prepared to wait for whatever the news was until later that afternoon.

'They no longer live with their mother,' Carol sighed. 'I knew they'd eventually discover what she's really like.'

'So what do they want, Carol?'

'They want to see me.'

'So they've forgiven you all of a sudden?'

'For God's sake, Sam!' Carol chewed her lip. It was all such a shock and her mind was in a whirl. 'Callum said his mother poisoned them against me. The fact their father wanted to live life as a woman was such a shock that they didn't know how to deal with it and believed everything she said. Now they're old enough to make up their own minds they want to re-establish our relationship.'

'I see.'

As Carol suspected, Sam wasn't taking the news very well.

'Here, read the letter.' She passed it to him and remained silent. She'd already had her sex change when she'd met Sam. For him it was love at first sight and although he was shocked when she told him on their second date, he still wanted to pursue a relationship. Before they married they both agreed that Carol's past life as Mark would remain in the past. Carol still recalled the conversation. She was happy to forget about her miserable life when she was trapped in a man's body. She always thought that if the boys contacted her, she would meet them somewhere in private and be able to keep that part of her life separate from her life with Sam. How naive, she now thought as he looked up from the letter.

'You must be thrilled. I know how much you miss them, even though you don't talk about it.'

So he did understand.

'Thanks, Sam. I'll phone Callum and tell him. I can't wait. It's going to be...'

'It's going to be great for you all. You'll have to arrange some time away of course but that shouldn't be a problem. Maybe I'll meet them too, but it will probably be better during another visit.'

97

'What do you mean *some time away*? Didn't you read the letter? They want to come here.'

'Don't you remember what we agreed, Carol? I love you more than anything but as Carol, not Mark. I don't want us to be the ones the local gossips talk about.'

'You mean you don't want your football mates taking the mickey because you're married to someone who used to be a bloke!'

'It's a big deal for me, Carol, but you knew that and we talked about it. You agreed!' he shouted the last then stormed into the kitchen. Sam ran the cold-water tap and took a drink, trying to calm down. 'Why do your boys have to come here? Does it really matter where you meet?'

'You just don't get it, Sam, do you?'

He shrugged.

'How can I expect my boys to embrace the fact their father's a woman and not feel any shame or embarrassment, when my own husband isn't willing to do so?'

Sam didn't answer.

'I'm going to the tournament.' Carol made sure she had everything in her bag and picked it up, along with her keys. 'Have a good day at the football and perhaps we can talk about this later?'

'Whatever,' he said, sounding like a stroppy teenager as she closed the door behind her.

*****

Marsha had trained hard during the summer. She was still overwhelmed with guilt about her feelings following Keith's death and netball was the release she needed. She'd lost weight and was fitter and healthier than she'd ever been. The tournament marking the beginning of the winter league would take place the following Saturday. She'd received many compliments at the last training session and had firmly secured her place as Goal Keeper for the Jaguars. As far as she could see, all the players were looking forward to the day except Penny, who had hardly said a word and was more aloof than usual. She let Penny's behaviour wash over her. Keith's death had taught her what was important in life and if someone had a bad attitude it was their problem not hers. Saying that, Rose's caustic observations could still upset her but she knew she wasn't alone in that respect.

98

'Have you got your lunch box, love?' Her mother-in-law asked.

Marsha checked her bag. 'Yes, thanks.'

'Your towel and your drinks?'

'I've got everything, Ann. I am thirty you know.'

Both women laughed. Ann enjoyed fussing over Marsha and her daughter in law loved the novelty of someone looking out for her.

'What are your plans for today?' asked Marsha.

'Well Colin is visiting his grand kids so I'm going to have a nice relaxing day on my own. I might even do a bit of gardening and watch a boxset, after I've made our dinner.'

'Ooh, that sounds good.'

'The boxset or dinner?'

'Both actually,' she said. 'What are we having?'

'It's a surprise.'

'I love surprises.'

Carol beeped her horn so Marsha said goodbye, picked up her bag and headed for the door. Dinner wouldn't be the only surprise that day. Despite all her hard work to get ready for it, Marsha would discover that this tournament wouldn't be remembered for the netball.

*****

She'd moved to the city when she finally accepted her pregnancy. Too far gone, she couldn't get rid of it. Although her first, she knew it was an unusual pregnancy. If her periods were anything to go by, she was over six months gone and the baby hardly showed; but for the occasional movement she would have been able to keep on denying it. She rented a small room in a house from a woman who liked to be called Mrs Willows and the landlady left her to her own devices. Her singing gave her enough to live on and a little over. She'd learnt to be careful, putting any extra money away knowing she wouldn't be able to earn money singing in clubs when the baby did start to show. She couldn't wait to get it out of her so she could get on with her life. Still angry with Keith for letting her down by dying, she didn't want any reminders of what could have been. There was no need to look in the mirror to know there was extra weight, but there still wasn't a massive bump. Most of her clothes no longer fitted. She didn't look her best and knew it so bought a few items from a charity shop and inexpensive retailer. There was no way she could

99

perform in these clothes so wasn't surprised when she lost her job. She told the club manager she thought she was coming down with something.

'You've got a great voice, love. Feel free to come back when you're, umm, feeling better and when you've bought a few new outfits. Okay?'

The next job was cash in hand cleaning but it only lasted a few weeks. She'd never been enthusiastic about her proper cleaning job and this one was no different. The rent was paid until the end of the month. She'd been frugal so there was enough to pay for another anonymous B&B after the baby was born. And enough to live on, for now. With no idea when it was due she could only hope it was soon. Pregnancy sucked!

It came sooner than expected. Mrs Willows didn't know she'd finished work, so she'd been out of the house all day. She'd wandered around the shops that morning then had a cup of tea and egg on toast in the late afternoon, in the local greasy spoon. The busy lunchtime trade had long gone so they didn't mind her sitting there for a few hours after. A wave of pain gripped her and she knew it was time. Leaving as soon as the pain subsided, she made her way back to her lodgings. Mrs Willows had been shopping and arrived at the house at the same time. One look at her lodger told her something was wrong.

'Are you all right, dear?'

She said she was but her landlady wasn't convinced as she watched her heavy tenant dragging herself upstairs to her room, clearly in pain. Mrs Willows heard nothing until the early hours of the morning when the screams and shouts woke her, and a very unhappy Mr Parsons, her other tenant.

Unconcerned about the girl's obvious pain, he demanded a rent refund. Mrs Willows wasn't in the mood. 'Please just go back to bed and let me sort things out.'

He was still chuntering as he left her to it. Mrs Willows opened the door. The girl was on all fours facing the door, thankfully, as her skimpy nightdress was pulled up around her waist. Her face was beetroot coloured with the strain of pushing. Their eyes met and Mrs Willows recognised the fear.

'Oh my dear Lord!' I'll get help.

'Don't leave me, please,' she said between pants.

'The doctor's only two doors up. I won't be long.'

She rushed out of the room, directly into Mr Parsons. 'Is she okay?'

'No, she's not. Go and fetch Doctor Fieldman. He's two up at number thirteen. Tell him we need him straight away.'

He was about to say something but she cut him short. 'Well go, on man. Tell him it's an emergency. She's having a baby.'

It did the trick and Mr Parsons moved as fast as his short, elderly legs would allow.

Mrs Willows was in the room with her when the doctor arrived, gripping her hand as she pushed with all her might. The baby's head was showing. It wasn't the first he'd delivered and Doctor Fieldman went calmly about his business. Twenty minutes later she gave birth to a healthy but small baby boy.

'I'll call an ambulance.'

She overhead the doctor speaking to her landlady.

'Please just let me sleep. I'll go to the hospital in the morning.'

She pointed to a bag at the bottom of her bed. 'His stuff's in there.'

They could see the girl was exhausted. Mrs Willows looked at the doctor. 'Is he okay?'

'He's a perfectly healthy baby, but he should really be checked out at the hospital.'

'Thanks, Doctor Fieldman, you're right. I'll call as soon as you leave and thanks again.' Mrs Willows rushed him out of the room then cleaned and dressed the baby before looking at the girl. She was already in a deep sleep. Mrs Willows didn't know what the matter was with people these days. In her day home births were common but women went to hospital if the midwife thought there'd be problems. It wouldn't do any harm to let her have a night's uninterrupted sleep; she wouldn't have many of those during the following weeks and months. She checked on the baby who was now sleeping peacefully, then closed the door quietly and left them to it.

By the time Mrs Willows got up in the morning to check on mother and baby, they'd disappeared.

Towards the end of the following week she knew motherhood wasn't everything it was cracked up to be and she was going stir crazy in her new room. She'd paid for a week and now the soreness had gone she felt perfectly well, but very fat and tired. By the time she left she hadn't bonded with the baby and knew he would be the bane of her life if she kept him, so she left the room and made her way to Keith's mothers.

Soon she would be free.

*****

Ann decided to prepare the dinner as soon as Marsha left, so the rest of the day was her own. She found the recipe for the one-pot beef stew and gave a wry smile as she wondered why they were called one-pot when there were always four or five to wash. *Sweet Caroline* was on the radio and she sang along as she gathered the ingredients and utensils from the fridge, cupboards and drawers.

Marsha had only been gone for a few minutes when there was a loud rap on the back door.

'What the heck,' she said out loud, not expecting anyone. The back door opened onto the small garden then backed onto a field that led to the countryside. Visitors rarely used that door.

She heard a baby crying as she left the kitchen and went to investigate. Her nervousness disappeared as the visitor rapped again.

'Okay, okay, I'm coming.'

Ann opened the door and looked at the girl thinking she was probably in her early twenties.

'Can I come in?' the visitor raised her voice to be heard over the infant's screams.

'I don't know you,' said Ann. 'I'm not well off so if it's money you're after...'

'I'm not a bloody gypo,' said the visitor. 'Keith was your son right?'

'Yes.'

'Well this little bundle of fun is your grandson!'

'What...?' Ann's right hand flew to her mouth and she used her left to grip the door and steady herself. 'But that can't be right, he was married to Marsha. Why would you say such a thing?' But as she said the words, Ann knew they'd both suspected her son of having an affair.

'We loved each other. He was going to leave *her*,' she said the word with venom. 'We planned to start our new life together then he went and died.'

She sobbed as she held out the baby to Ann who took him and cradled him, making cooing noises as she did so. The

102

baby stopped crying and gripped her little finger. Her visitor spoke before she had a chance to look at her grandson properly.

'Can I come in then or what?' she said as she picked up the bag she'd also brought with her.

Ann led her into the lounge where they both sat down. She spent a moment looking at the baby boy who had now stopped crying and was sleeping peacefully. He was very young but looked exactly as Keith had at that age. Her heart surged with love.

'Who are you?'

'Any chance of a cuppa?' she answered, ignoring Ann's question. 'And I wouldn't say no to a bacon butty.'

'You can't come into my house telling me I have a grandson then demanding breakfast. Who do you think you are?'

'Sorry,' said the visitor. Ann could see she didn't really mean it. 'I haven't eaten for a while and I'm starving.'

Taking pity on her she went to give the baby back to his mother before heading for the kitchen.

'Just put him on the sofa.'

She did as asked. Her emotions were raw as she prepared the tea and sandwich. She would need to get to know her visitor so she could have regular contact with her grandson. Ann was already looking forward to watching him grow up, imagining days out at the zoo with Colin and the little one when he was a bit older. This was turning out to be the best day since Keith had died. Her son would live on in his child. It would be upsetting for Marsha of course, but she was a lovely girl and she'd get used to it, eventually.

She buttered the bread as she daydreamed about the future. The back door banging brought her back to the present. Ann rushed into the room. The visitor had left without her son. She ran to the back door and opened it. There was no sign of the woman. She had to have run over the field or was hiding somewhere. She couldn't leave the baby alone to look for her, but if she took him with her, the woman would be long gone. Distressed, Ann returned to the living room. The baby was sleeping, totally oblivious to the fact that his mother abandoned him. She noticed an envelope on the sofa next to him with the word *grandmother* on the front. Then she saw her open purse on the coffee table, now empty where the notes had been. She ignored the purse and tore open the letter. Reading the contents Ann put her hand to her mouth for the second time that day. The baby was in a deep sleep. Her hand was shaking as she phoned Colin who said he'd make arrangements for his grand kids and be over as soon as he could.

*****

Carol had hardly said a word so it was obvious something was wrong. 'What's happened?' asked Marsha?

She didn't answer for a few seconds.

'Carol?'

'I need to talk to you. Do you mind being a bit late for the tournament?'

'Of course not.'

Carol indicated and turned down a side street. She found a quiet area to park.

'This mustn't go any further. Do you understand?'

'You know you can trust me, Carol.'

'I do, Marsha but this isn't run of the mill stuff and people react differently.'

'For God's sake what on earth is it?'

'I'll also understand if you don't want to be friends anymore too.'

'Are you a serial killer or something?' Marsha tried to make a joke of it but neither laughed.

'I used to be a man.'

'Ha ha, very funny. What is it really?' she said, then saw the look on Carol's face. 'Aah.'

'Shit, Carol. I'm sorry. I didn't mean to make a joke of it, it's just that... Well what I'm trying to say is...'

Carol stopped her from digging any further holes. 'It's okay, Marsha. I can see it must have come as quite a shock for you.'

'Gross understatement but, yes, you're right. How long were you a... I mean what made you decide to ermm, you know?'

'I was a woman trapped in a man's body. For most of my life I denied it, then there came a point where I couldn't deny it any longer. It was just over five years ago when I made the decision. The hardest of my life. My then wife went berserk, turned against me and turned my teenage boys against me too.'

'How awful. So why now? What's happened for you to tell me about this now?'

104

Carol explained the agreement she had with Sam and the letter from Callum. 'I miss them so much, you just can't imagine,' she looked at her friend. 'Scrub that, I know you can imagine exactly how much I miss them.'

'I can and if there's anything I can do to help you in any way, you know you only have to ask.'

'Thanks, Marsha. That means a lot to me.'

Marsha leaned over and gave her friend an awkward hug.

Carol shook her head when they parted. 'I'm stuck between the people I love. I don't know what to do.'

'I think you do, Carol. Deep in your heart you know exactly what to do but you're terrified Sam will leave you.'

She was absolutely right. Carol gave a wry smile and turned the engine back on. 'Come on, let's go and play netball. I know I'm going to see my sons again, the rest can wait until after the tournament.'

*****

It was the usual location. The weather was reasonably good for September. It was forecast to be overcast, but dry, so they were able to play on the outside courts. Many players headed for the changing rooms following the warm-up to do whatever they had to prior to the start of the matches.

Penny was warming up on court when she realised that people were looking at her. One girl from another team whispered something to a teammate, pointed in Penny's direction then they both sniggered. They stopped and looked away as soon as Penny looked directly at them. What on earth was going on? Looking toward her own team benches she could see that Kaitlyn had arrived and was with Sandy. Carol was talking to them and from this distance, it looked like the conversation was heated. People were gathering around Carol, Kaitlyn and Sandy as Penny made her way towards them, wondering what was going on.

She heard part of the conversation as she approached.

'Don't do this to her,' said Carol. 'This is private, Kaitlyn, between you and your family.'

'She should have thought of that before she shagged my husband.'

Sandy's words stopped Penny in her tracks as she realised her secret was out. She quickly recovered her composure but it was too late. Onlookers had seen the truth on her face.

105

Penny wanted to escape but her feet felt rooted to the spot. She watched as Kaitlyn unfurled the large scroll she held.

'Kaitlyn?' then. 'How could you?' said Penny as she looked at it in horror. There was a photograph of her on the scroll. She was lying naked on the bed, eyes closed with a satisfied post-coital smile on her face.

'This must be just after my husband gave you a seeing to,' said Sandy. 'How could you, Penny?' Sandy was already humiliated, knowing that everyone would soon know about the affair but it didn't matter. She wouldn't see them again. The stuck up cow had helped to ruin her marriage and she wanted payback 'Have you no shame?'

'I don't know who took that, but it's not what you think.'

'Well I know Daddy didn't take it,' said Kaitlyn.

'And I found it on my husband's phone,' Sandy added. 'Do you need any more clues?'

Penny couldn't stand it any longer. She turned and the small crowd parted as she ran to the changing rooms to collect her kit bag. 'Damn you Kaitlyn,' she said as she saw copies of the same photograph dotted around the walls of the room. Believing she couldn't feel any worse she was proved wrong as her phone pinged. Kaitlyn had tagged her in a Facebook post entitled *What Mummy does in her spare time*. Oh my God! So that's why her daughter had sent her a friend request. Penny ran to her car and drove. On the way home she stopped in a layby and checked her notifications. It was all over social media with a number of unsavoury comments. Through her tears she spent some time unfriending her daughter and teammates. She had to get away as quickly as possible. Arriving at the mansion she planned to pack and move to their villa in Spain until the fuss died down. Paul must have put their daughter up to this. Penny was going to contact her solicitor and get as much out of her husband as possible. Much as she hated Kaitlyn at the moment, she knew she had to use the prostitution as a bargaining chip with Paul, so outing her daughter was not an option. She would have to get her revenge some other way. When the dust settled she'd make her husband and bitch of a daughter pay.

The key didn't fit the door. It didn't take long for her to realise she'd been locked out. Penny ran to her car and headed for the bank on the High Street, receiving some funny looks as she was still in her short netball skirt and top. Her fears were confirmed as she keyed in the pin number twice to no avail. She smiled to herself. *Did he think she was completely stupid?* Taking out the card for the account she'd opened shortly after Paul had told her he knew about her affairs, she keyed in the pin. Success. The thousands were still in her single account and there was no way he could get his hands on that money. She planned to stay in London for the rest of the weekend and visit the passport office first thing Monday morning. It would be a bore queuing with the hoi polloi but there was no way she could face either of them.

But first, some new clothes.

*****

'Where's Penny?' asked Rose. Carol and Marsha gave her a look as if she'd just arrived from outer space.

'Didn't you see what happened?' asked Carol.

'Of course, but I never thought Penny would let the team down.'

'Are you for real?' Marsha didn't wait for an answer as she grabbed a ball and followed Chardonnay and the others. She'd had her fill of drama for one day. As they passed the ball around she marvelled at the calmness of Sandy and Kaitlyn. Especially Sandy. They must have been planning the day's showdown for some time she thought.

'Suzanne?' they turned as they heard Rose say the name. 'What are you doing here?'

Here we go again, thought Marsha. *Never a dull moment with this lot.*

'I thought I'd come and watch,' said Suzanne.

As Rose wondered if Suzanne would be able to play, Chardonnay marched over to her sister. 'Oh My God,' she said, standing in front of her with her hands on her hips. 'You disappear for months then just turn up to spectate, as if nothing has happened?'

'Don't exaggerate, Chardonnay. I told Mum I was going away to work for a while so it's not like I disappeared off the face of the earth.'

'Well where have you been?'

Suzanne ignored her sister and turned to speak to Rose. Chardonnay was having none of it. 'You couldn't have been working very hard by the size of you.'

Suzanne snapped around. 'You cheeky cow. Who do you...' she was about to lay into her when she saw the smug look

107

on Chardonnay's face and others waiting to hear their argument. She decided to change tack. 'I haven't been well but I'm better now and starting to lose the weight I gained.'

'Are you okay?'

She could play her sister like a fiddle. Suzanne kept her sad expression and nodded. 'I'll tell you all about it later.'

Seeing Chardonnay fall for her sister's bullshit, Marsha and Carol rolled their eyes at each other. Rose was her usual business-like self. 'Are you back for good?' she asked.

'I'm moving on,' She ensured that everybody heard. 'I've accepted a job on a cruise ship. My singing career is really taking off. Move over Jane McDonald.'

They'd heard similar boasts before so most of her teammates took her news with a pinch of salt. Not the reaction she had hoped for.

'Are you able to play?' asked Rose.

'I'm fine now, so can if you want me to.'

'You're in the team.' Rose rummaged in the big kit bag. 'Here, these are the biggest. They should just about fit you, but it'll be a squeeze.'

Subtle thought Marsha as she rolled her eyes at Carol again.

Suzanne flicked her hair back diva style, picked up the netball kit and sauntered towards the changing rooms.

'Exit stage left,' muttered Marsha louder than she'd intended. Those within hearing distance chuckled.

As her sister went off to change, Chardonnay called her mother. They hung up with her promising to try to bring her sister home with her.

Without any further drama the tournament kicked off.

*****

Despite the pre-netball dramatics, it was a fun day and Rose was glowing as she said her goodbyes following the prize giving and tidying up. Her team had won so all was well in her world.

'No training for two weeks girls, so enjoy the break. I'll put a reminder on the Facebook Group for the following week.'

Marsha was amazed Carol had carried on as normal throughout the day. When she had a quiet word, Carol said she didn't want anyone else knowing her business, especially some of the netball team. 'I know they're mates but this lot love a good

108

gossip.' Marsha was honoured that Carol put her trust in her. She wouldn't let her down.

When they were ready to leave, Carol offered to drop Suzanne off with Chardonnay.

'Thanks but I'm going back to my flat.'

'But I thought you'd moved out of your flat?' Chardonnay said.

'Okay it's not technically mine but I'm staying with a friend.'

'Who?' asked Chardonnay. Trying to get to the bottom of her sister's porkies.

'What is this? The bloody Spanish Inquisition? I don't want a lift okay.'

'What shall I tell Mum?'

'Tell her I'll phone her tonight,' she gave her sister a warning look. 'Have you finished with the interrogation now?'

Seeing their exchange could turn into a full-scale argument, Carol interrupted.

'Shall we make a move?'

Suzanne left them to it as Carol, Marsha and Chardonnay headed for the car.

Marsha put a friendly arm around Chardonnay's shoulder. She couldn't stand Suzanne and was glad she'd declined a lift, but she could see Chardonnay was upset.

'Are you all right?'

'I'll be fine thanks, Marsha. I don't know why she's such a cow to me when I was only trying to be nice? She disappears for months on end then kicks off when all I did was to ask her a reasonable question.'

'Try not to let it upset you. She said she's been ill so maybe she's still not feeling well. If something's wrong we usually lash out at those closest to us.'

'Maybe you're right. But why is that?'

'No idea,' said Marsha, 'but if I ever find out I'll let you know.' She gave Chardonnay a squeeze and was rewarded with a smile.

Despite the events of the day, they were on a high after winning the tournament. They'd picked the bones off the goings on beforehand and worn the subject out. Carol appeared to be in good spirits considering her earlier revelations. Marsha was full of beans on the way home in Carol's car, relieved that her friend was holding up well, and that Suzanne wasn't with them. The fact that they'd won also made her feel good. She sang along to the Rag N Bone Man CD.

'*I'm only human after all, I'm only human after all, don't put the blame on me... Oh yeah. Don't put the blame on me...*'

'It's a good job you're not singing on any cruise ship,' said Chardonnay. 'They'd all throw themselves overboard.'

The three laughed which set the tone for the rest of the journey.

*****

As Sandy returned home following the tournament she was grateful that Leon was on overnight duty at the barracks. She corrected herself, assuming he was actually on duty and not seeing some other woman. Kaitlyn knew she was leaving but not the others. She'd made the right decision about getting it out in the open. The girls had been supportive and the only one likely to be horrible was Suzanne, but Sandy didn't plan on seeing her again, nor the others for that matter. There'd been enough emotion for one day and she'd be long gone by the time they started training in a few weeks. By then she'd be licking her wounds on her lovely island but would have the comfort and love of her children and parents to help her get through it. She packed her bags then confirmed her international bank transfer online. She didn't feel any guilt about taking all the money out of their joint account and the savings account in her own name. The long flight was expensive but she'd got a good deal and with that amount of money, she could live very well in Fiji for some time. She would wait until she was properly settled, then decide what to do for the best for their future. As much as she loved her husband she couldn't forgive him so it was over. She considered writing him a letter but that was the coward's way. Sandy slept fitfully, not looking forward to saying goodbye to Leon the following morning.

*****

Kaitlyn had showered and changed and headed directly to the restaurant for dinner with her father.

Paul placed their order and she watched the waiter leave before speaking. 'Can I talk to you about Sandy?'

'Sandy?' He tried to remember who she was.

'The wife of the Fijian man that Mummy, err...'

'Of course. I should have remembered.'

110

'She's the innocent victim in all of this, Daddy. She's lost her home and has to return to Fiji.'

'Why?'

'She's leaving her husband and although the military could help her, she doesn't want to be anywhere near him. Her mother looks after their kids in Fiji, but they were saving as much as they could so they could bring the kids over to live with them. She wanted her mother to come too so Sandy could still work, but her husband wouldn't allow it.'

'He wouldn't allow it? That's a bit...'

'It doesn't matter, Daddy. She's going to tell him their marriage is over and she's leaving him.'

'I see.' It was unfortunate, but Sandy was collateral damage. He felt sorry for the woman but it was better for her to find out sooner rather than later what her husband was really like.

'As I said, Sandy is the innocent victim in all of this.'

It clicked and Paul could now see where Kaitlyn was heading.

'So you want me to help her?'

'Yes please.'

She pleaded with her eyes and his heart melted.

'What can she do?'

'She worked in an office but is easy-going, fun to be around and knows the value of money. With a bit of training I think she could manage one of your shops.'

'Oh you do, do you?' Paul folded his arms and tried not to laugh as his daughter outlined her plan.

'I know she won't want to live in Bloomington, so if you could set her up in a house that's big enough for her to live in with her mother and kids and give her a job, that would be great.'

'And what does Sandy have to say about all of this?'

'DOH! I haven't spoken to her, obviously. I would never take your generous nature for granted.'

Now Paul did laugh and Kaitlyn pretended to look hurt before joining in with him.

'Okay, I suppose you're right. She is the innocent one in all of this. Speak to her and tell her she'll need to be flexible. I'll let you know where we'll place her and I'll get Brian to sort out the paperwork. We'll have something for her by the time she's ready to return from Fiji.'

111

'Thanks, Daddy. You're the best.' She got up and gave him a kiss.

Their Chateaubriand arrived and they ate in silence for a few minutes, enjoying the tender steak.

Kaitlyn broke the silence. 'So where will Mummy go?'

'Probably to Spain, darling.' He'd taken some satisfaction about the humiliation of his wife but would have preferred a different ending.

She noticed the faraway look in his eyes. Putting down her cutlery she placed a hand on her father's to regain his attention.

'What's wrong?'

'Nothing, darling.'

'I'm not a child anymore. After all we've been through you should know you can trust me. What is it?'

Paul sighed. 'I still love her. It's crazy after everything she's done to me... everything we've done to each other and I don't like your mother. But dammit,' he banged his fist on the table. 'I still love the bloody woman.'

'Poor Daddy. What are you going to do?'

'Work hard. That always helps to take my mind off things.'

Giving a sympathetic smile Kaitlyn planned to work hard too. To find her father someone he could trust and would love him for who he was and not what he was worth.

*****

Carol dropped Chardonnay off, then Marsha a little later. Marsha was still singing as she put the key in the lock. The smell hit her straight away and she was instantly transported to the time when she held her baby daughter in her arms, before they'd come to take her away. A baby's crying brought her back to the present. She took in the scene. The baby, most definitely a boy, was lying on a towel on the floor and Ann was crooning over him as she changed his nappy. Colin was looking at Ann and the baby. He had a small towel thrown over one shoulder and his shirtsleeves were rolled up.

'What's going on here? And who's this little fella?'

Ann quickly finished what she was doing. The baby stopped crying as soon as she hugged him to her breast.

'Are you babysitting?'

112

Ann took a deep breath, knowing how important it was to get this right.

Ann?'

She passed her grandson to Marsha, whose heart surged as soon as she held the warm infant to her chest. Closing her eyes she inhaled the smell and feel of him. There was nothing else like it. He made a cute gurgling noise then closed his eyes and was asleep within seconds.

Ann looked at her daughter-in-law's reaction. So far so good.

'He was left on the doorstep, Marsha, with a note asking me to look after him.'

'What!? This is the twenty-first century, Ann. That sort of thing doesn't happen.'

'It's exactly what did happen though. Isn't he just gorgeous?'

'What did Social Services say? When are they coming for him?'

'I'll make a cuppa then I'll get off,' said Colin. 'Then you can tell Marsha everything.'

Marsha was only half listening as she reveled in the scent and feel of the baby. 'How could anyone abandon this little fella? He's adorable.'

Colin took his leave and Marsha reluctantly settled the baby on the settee. She took a sip of her tea. 'So what did Social Services say, Ann?'

'We've to keep Daniel here overnight and they'll come tomorrow.'

Marsha knew she was lying. 'So his name's Daniel?'

Ann smiled her agreement. 'Shall we go out tomorrow and buy him everything he needs?'

She looked at Daniel then at her mother-in-law. Could they really get away with it? Trying not to think too far ahead she made her decision.

'Yes. Let's do that.'

*****

Chardonnay let herself into the house following the tournament. 'I'm home, Mum.'

Her mother rushed down the stairs. 'Is Suzanne with you?'

Great to see you too, Mum. 'No. She said she'd call you.'

113

'But you promised, Chardonnay.'

Here we go again. Always taking the blame for Suzanne.
'I promised I'd try, Mum, and I did. But Suzanne wouldn't come.'

'Well why on earth not, and how is she?'

Chardonnay looked at her mother's concerned face and didn't want to cause her further worry. 'She's fine, honestly. I don't know what's going on in her life but I'm sure she'll tell you when she calls. I'm off for my shower.' Chardonnay disappeared before her mother could interrogate her further.

Suzanne didn't call until the Sunday. Chardonnay had spent as much time out of the house as she could to avoid her mother's incessant questions. Her father thought it hilarious that his daughter went fishing with him the following day. She hated fishing but they both wanted a break from all the talk of Suzanne.

It had been so long since she'd spent time alone with her father. They enjoyed each other's company and had a lovely day. Returning to the house they were in good spirits.

'She's going away again, Mike.'

He rolled his eyes at Chardonnay who disappeared to the kitchen to make a brew.

'Oh, Hazel. Calm down, love and tell me what's happened this....' he stopped himself from saying this time, knowing that would upset his wife.

'She said everything's fine and that she really has got a singing job. She's going to be based in Spain. But I'm not sure I believe her.'

Their daughter had lied before so they were both skeptical. 'When is she going?'

'On Wednesday.'

Chardonnay had heard the conversation and returned with the tea. 'So I'll probably see her at netball in a few weeks then.'

Her father smirked.

'It's just a big joke to you two isn't it?'

'No it's not. The main thing is she's fine. She's almost twenty-one and if she wants to go off and do her own thing, we can't stop her. It would be nice to see her or at least speak to her before she goes away though, just so I know she's okay.'

'She wants to speak to you before she goes too. She's coming round for her tea on Tuesday night.'

114

'I'll make sure I finish work early then,' said Mike. 'And we'll have a nice family tea together.'

'Can't wait,' said Chardonnay before dodging the cushion her father threw at her.

Chapter 13

'I'm home,' shouted Leon as he unlocked the front door. He expected Sandy to be up to make him breakfast but couldn't smell anything as he entered the kitchen. 'Sandy?' he called. Starting to feel annoyed that she wasn't where she should be. He heard banging on the stairs and went into the passage to investigate. 'What the hell?'

Sandy was lugging a suitcase down the stairs and was dressed to go out, even though it was only eight o'clock. Leon watched, his mind trying to work out what was going on.

'The hell is, I'm leaving.' She placed her case in the hallway, leaving enough room to open the front door.

'What do you mean you're leaving?'

Looking at her husband, Sandy couldn't believe he didn't get it.

'Do I have to spell it out to you? You had an affair, I found out about it and don't want to be married to you any more. Understand?'

'No. You are my wife. You can't leave. And I haven't had an affair.'

She couldn't believe he acted like the injured party when he had ruined their marriage. 'Leon. I know about your affair. I followed you to London and know you stayed in a plush hotel with a rich woman, while I was trying to save all our pennies so we could have our babies with us.'

'But, Sandy. You don't understand.'

'What's there to understand? You slept with another woman, which tells me our marriage vows mean nothing to you. I'm not going to be one of those women who turn a blind eye. I am your equal, whether you like it or not and I'm going home.' She didn't tell him that she would return to work for Kaitlyn's father. That could wait. Sandy went to open the door but he put a hand on her arm to stop her.

'I did it for us, Sandy. They paid me. I took the money so we could see our babies sooner.'

'That's even worse,' she unpeeled his hand from her arm. 'You took our vows so lightly that you thought it would be okay to...' she searched for the right words. 'You more or less prostituted yourself and justified it by using our children as an

116

excuse. I don't love you any more. In fact, Leon, you disgust me.' She wanted to spit in his face but resisted the urge.

'You are my wife and you are not going anywhere!' he raised his hand. Sandy took a step back towards the stairs.

'You can threaten me with violence and even if I end up in hospital, I will still leave you. It's over, Leon.'

The realisation finally registered and he slumped down the wall to sit on the floor. He loved her but didn't have it in him to beg her to stay.

Sandy's lips were quivering but she was determined not to cry. She climbed over his legs and opened the door. Picking up the case she took one last look at her husband and left, closing the door behind her.

Leon went to the kitchen and took the grog out of the cupboard. He took a deep swig of the liquid straight from the bottle. The sooner he reached oblivion, the better.

*****

Marsha phoned in sick on the Monday. 'Some sort of bug I think,' she coughed into the phone.

'Poor you,' said Sasha. 'You're right not to come in. Don't want you spreading your germs on the customers. But looking on the bright side there's no netball for a few weeks so at least you won't miss any training sessions.'

The important things in life thought Marsha as she hung up the phone. While netball was a big deal, it was nothing compared to the new little man in their lives. The one who was currently crying at the top of his voice. Both Marsha and Ann headed in his direction. The phone rang so Marsha turned to answer it.

'Hi. How are you?' asked Carol.

'I'm hoping it's one of those forty eight hour things and I'll be back to work later in the week.'

Daniel cried as if the end of the world was coming.

'Who is that?' asked Carol.

'A friend of Ann's is here with her grandson, she's trying to settle him now. Sorry I need the loo, I've got to go.' Marsha hung up. She knew Carol would see through her lie and she would have to tell her friend eventually, but not just yet. She looked at Ann who was holding Daniel and cooing to him as she gently rocked him. Marsha had a reality check. The bubble of the last two days had suddenly burst and she admitted to herself that they would have to give him up. Perhaps they could apply to foster him, as his mother seemed to have disappeared from the face of the earth.

Ann looked at Marsha as if she could read her mind. She shook her head.

'I'm sorry, Ann. We have to give him up.'

'I'll never give him up, Marsha.' Even though her mouth said the words, her mind denied them and she started crying. Then uncontrollable sobs took over her whole body. Daniel joined in and so did Marsha. The women cried as if someone had died. Eventually cried out and exhausted, Ann put Daniel down for a sleep.

'I have something to tell you.'

Marsha knew it wasn't going to be good news.

'Sit down, love.' Ann took a deep breath knowing she had to tell her but dreading her reaction.

'What is it?' Her heart was racing but she didn't know why.

'You know I didn't know the girl who left the baby.'

'Yeah, you already told me that.'

'There's a few things I didn't tell you.'

'You've got me worried now, Ann. Whatever it is, please just spit it out.'

'Okay. The first one is she left me a note asking me to look after him and telling me she wouldn't be back.'

'Why didn't you mention that before? And why you?'

'I didn't mention it because the girl knew Keith. They were having an affair.' Ann watched as realisation dawned on Marsha's face.

'So Daniel... the baby... he's,' she started to shake. 'That little baby is a result of my dead husband's affair with that girl, whoever she is.'

'That's right, Marsha. I'm so sorry...'

'So he's your grandson? Right? Why didn't you tell me? How could you keep that from me, Ann?' She wasn't screaming or shouting, it might have been easier for Ann to cope with if she was. She was upset and looked at her mother-in-law as if she were a stranger.

She got up and headed towards the door.

'Where are you going?'

'I don't think that's any of your business, Ann.'

Marsha ran to her room, put on her shoes and a jacket then left the house. As she walked down the street she dialed Carol's office number.

'Can you talk?'

Carol put a *do not disturb* sign on her door and closed it.

'You sound upset.'

'That's an understatement,' said Marsha. She explained how she'd returned home to find a baby in the house and now Ann's revelation that he was her grandson.

'Whoah, whoah.' Carol was trying to get her head around all of the information. 'Poor you. But what did Social Services say? I'm surprised they didn't take him away straight away.'

'He's her grandson, Carol. I love the little mite already. How could Ann not tell me after all we've been through together? It's so unfair.'

Worried about her friend, Carol decided not to push her about calling the Social Services. Something wasn't right and she needed to speak to her in person.

'Where are you now?'

'Walking down the street. I couldn't face being in the same house as Ann so I had to get out.'

'Okay.' Carol looked at her watch. She had a meeting with her boss and colleagues within the next few minutes. 'I'll come as soon as I get out of my meeting. Where will you be?'

'I'm not sure, Carol. I need to clear my head and decide what I want to do. I'm going to walk for a bit and I'll call you later if that's okay?'

Although she still sounded upset, she did seem a little calmer. 'Okay. But you don't have to make any hasty decisions. Just remember that.'

After saying goodbye Marsha turned off her phone and walked.

An hour later her mind was clearer and she'd made her decision. As she put the key in the front door she knew the next weeks and months weren't going to be easy, for either of them.

'Marsha?' Ann sounded desperate.

'Oh thank God you've come back. I'm so sorry, really I am. I didn't want to upset you and wanted you to like Daniel.'

Marsha was about to speak but Ann stopped her. 'I know he's only a baby and there's no way you'd hold the circumstances of his birth against him, but it was all too much to take in and I couldn't cope with you being upset and trying to look after Daniel too.'

'Okay, Ann. Obviously I'm not happy that you didn't tell me, but I can sort of understand why,' she sighed. 'But where do we go from here? You know we have to tell Social Services don't you?'

'Yes, I know. But his own mother's abandoned him and I'm not prepared to do that too. I'm going to apply to adopt him.'

Marsha wasn't surprised. They'd both bonded with the infant and she also loved him, despite the circumstances of his arrival. She'd given up one baby against her will and she fully intended to help Ann fight for this one.

'Will you help me?'

She stopped daydreaming. 'Of course. But we need to phone Social Services. We'll tell them the baby was left today while I was out shopping, Ann. You can tell exactly the same story and just change the day. It's only a small lie and it could make a difference when it comes to your adoption application.'

It made sense to Ann and she agreed. 'But I'll have to tell Colin so he can back up my story.'

'Will he be all right with it?' asked Marsha.

Ann said he would. 'He'll be relieved that we've decided to call the authorities. Keeping Daniel without telling anyone didn't sit easy with him. I'll phone him now.'

'Before you do that. What if the girl lied to you and you're not really his grandmother?'

Ann smiled. 'There's no doubt in my mind.' She moved to the cupboard in the corner of the room and brought out a photo album. 'Look.'

Marsha leafed through the photos of Keith as a baby. They looked exactly alike.

'Okay, but they'll insist on doing a DNA test. You know that don't you?'

Ann didn't but now Marsha had told her, it made sense.

'There's no doubt in my mind.'

'Good.'

'One more thing,' said Ann. 'She didn't tell me his name was Daniel, but I've always liked that name...'

'Daniel it is then,' she said as Ann went to make the calls.

Carol and the Social Services arrived at the same time. Marsha gave Carol a warning look. 'A woman left the baby with Ann today, when I was out. She told her his name's Daniel and she's his grandmother.'

'I should imagine that was quite a shock,' said the Social Worker as she smiled sympathetically.

'Understatement,' said Ann.

She explained what would happen when she had all the details she needed. 'We'll put Daniel into Foster care and arrange for the DNA tests. Once it's confirmed that you are his grandmother, you can apply for custody. It's complicated because of his missing mother. I need to phone the police and they'll want to interview you.'

Ann burst into tears.

'I'll make a cuppa,' said Carol, reverting to her default setting whenever there was a drama with Marsha.

'I'm so sorry,' said Ann.

'You've got nothing to be sorry for,' the Social Worker tapped her hand. 'You've been told you're a grandmother and had a baby given to you and taken from you all in one day. You have every right to be upset.' She was careful not to use the word *grandson,* as there was no concrete evidence yet. 'Can you gather Daniel's things together please while I call the police?'

Ann and Marsha repeated the same story to the police. Colin had arrived by this time. He told his version of the story and the police had no need to disbelieve them. When they asked about the baby's mother Ann gave the best description that she could. They asked her to go to the station the following day to work with a photo-fit officer.

The story made the local news that evening with a plea for the baby's mother to come forward, and a number for the public to call if they had any information.

121

Chapter 14

Penny had settled into the villa they'd bought five years earlier. They had rented out the exclusive property on a short-term basis but, luckily, they'd been between tenants when she needed to move. She collected the keys from the agency and terminated their agreement. There had been no comebacks so Penny knew that Paul must have approved her actions. One less thing for them to fight about. It had been difficult at first while she licked her wounds but she forced herself to snap out of it. Being fit and healthy made her feel good about herself and Penny was proud that she had a figure of a much younger woman. She hadn't worked out in a few weeks and had started to feel lethargic. It was time to move on. She wanted to join a gym and find a netball team, if there was one. She knew netball wasn't played widely throughout Europe, but hoped there might be some sort of Expat league.

The following day while shopping in *Comida Gloriosa* - the supermarket that was as similar as she could find to Waitrose – the packing staff put a free magazine in her bag. After she put away her groceries, Penny noticed it was in English and flicked through it. It was a Godsend. *LEXI* was the local Expat magazine and was filled with information about clubs and activities. Thankfully, there was a netball scene with information about who to contact. She dialled the number.

'Hi, Amanda Brookes.'

Penny introduced herself. 'I've just moved here from the UK and am interested in playing.'

Amanda told her there was a small league and they played all year round. Outdoors in the winter and inside during the intense heat of the summer. 'Training's on tomorrow if you're interested? Let me know where you live and I'll give you directions.'

Penny explained that she lived in the exclusive Palm Tree Heights area, at *HighTops Villa*. Paul had chosen the unimaginative name and she was always embarrassed to tell people.

'You're kidding me? That's where I live, less than half a mile away. Fancy coming over for a coffee or something stronger?'

122

'I'd love to. I've been so busy since I arrived, I haven't had a chance to socialise.'

'How about an early dinner this evening? I'll get Bella to make her Paella. It's absolutely wonderful.'

The arrangements were made. When she hung up Penny started to feel a lot more optimistic. Amanda sounded like a woman after her own heart and she hoped they could be friends. She wasn't disappointed.

The door opened within seconds of the bell ringing. An older woman with olive skin, wearing three-quarter length trousers and a t-shirt told her to come in. She also beckoned with an arm in case Penny hadn't understood her heavily accented English. Penny guessed she must be Bella. She wondered is she was from the same agency as her own housekeeper, Sophia.

Penny looked around the sumptuous entranceway. The high ceiling had wooden beams and colourful paintings were hung on the walls. Object d'art were tastefully placed on one or two pieces of furniture. The whole area gave the impression of understated opulence.

'You must be Penny?'

She turned to the voice and watched as Amanda glided down the stairs and made her way towards her.

'Hello, sweetie. How lovely to meet you,' said Amanda.

She was dressed in casual denim shorts and vest over a bikini top. Penny felt overdressed in her linen dress and jewellery. She guessed Amanda was a similar age to her but noticed she'd had work done too, so it was hard to tell. She had a lovely trim figure so it was obvious she kept herself fit.

'You too,' said Penny and they air kissed on both cheeks.

'Wine or shall we have champers, to celebrate your arrival?'

'Champagne would be marvellous thanks.'

Amanda nodded to Bella who disappeared to get the drinks.

'Let's go to the garden,' she said and Penny followed.

The outside was as tasteful as the inside and they relaxed at a table in the shaded area around the pool.

Penny explained she'd recently broken up with her husband.

'Welcome to the club,' said Amanda as she gave a sympathetic smile. 'Mine's long gone. The bastard traded me in

123

for a younger model. God knows why?' She shrugged her shoulders then ran her hands down the outside of her body, looking genuinely surprised at how anyone could leave her.

Penny laughed.

'But there's plenty of action here to keep me busy, and you if you want it, sweetie?' She winked and Penny knew they would become firm friends.

*****

It was a short drive to the gymnasium and netball courts so Amanda arranged to pick Penny up the following evening. She was all business in the car on the way.

'So we currently have two teams in the club, which can go up to three in the winter. You know, the people who visit to get away from the dreadful winters at home. Our ages range from late teens to women in their fifties, and there's the usual mix of those who get on with each other and those who don't. But they're generally a friendly bunch.'

Penny listened quietly as Amanda continued. 'We had one newbie last week. She works out here as a singer apparently but I've never heard of her. Anyway, sweetie, she's not like you and I.'

Penny nodded. 'So do you need shooters?'

'We always need shooters, sweetie. I've had to play Shooter for the last two matches, but I hate it. I only did it to keep the peace as Melanie is such a diva and will only play Goal Attack.'

'I see.'

Amanda parked up and they headed into the building. This is more like it, thought Penny as she looked around the modern reception area. If the rest of the place was as well looked after, she would be very happy. They'd agreed that Penny would decide whether to join the club following her first session, but she'd already decided to join the gym. She filled out the required forms and gave the pleasant receptionist her credit card. Following payment she was allocated a locker and followed Amanda into the female changing rooms.

There were only a few others in the changing rooms and she did a double take as she recognised the first person she saw.

Suzanne got in first. 'Well, well, well. Fancy seeing you here.'

124

'What are you doing here?' She looked a lot slimmer and fitter than last time Penny had seen her.

'I'm a singer now and I work here.'

'Of course you do,' said Penny. 'Is that before or after you've cleaned the hotel rooms?'

'You cheeky cow.' Suzanne was furious. 'You've got no right to be so stuck up after the way you treated Sandy and the rest of them. I bet nobody here knows do they? Well we'll soon see about that...

'Ladies, ladies, please,' Amanda interrupted. 'Let's concentrate on the netball and sort out our differences after training.' She was intrigued and looking forward to hearing what Penny had to say later.

Penny had expected the netball to be a casual set-up; she was wrong. Suzanne's apparent new best friend Melanie took the warm up which was more intense than she was used to, but Amanda directed proceedings. They did circuit training for thirty minutes before doing any netball drills, followed by a mini-match. After the circuits Penny saw Suzanne whispering to Melanie and nodding in her direction. She thought she was coming to Spain for a clean start but everyone would soon know her past if Suzanne had her way. Anger fuelled her netball and Penny played better than she had in ages. Amanda was impressed and told her so during the drive home.

'You're definitely first-team standard. I'll have a word with Melanie. Give her the choice of playing Wing Attack or if she wants to shoot, Goal Attack for the second team.'

'I shouldn't bother,' said Penny. 'I won't be coming back.'

'I'd rather you play for us than Suzanne. And anyway, sweetie, she won't be there every week because of her singing.'

'She's been going on about her singing for ages but it's never happened,' Penny harrumphed. 'So if you believe that now you'll believe anything.'

'Okay, but if she gossips she's going to do it whether you're there or not.'

'But what I did was pretty awful, Amanda.'

'What? Getting caught?'

They laughed and Penny felt better. 'I had an affair with a husband of one of our players. My daughter and the wife displayed naked photographs of me at the last tournament, then

125

confronted me. And if that wasn't bad enough, my daughter Kaitlyn also posted them on Facebook.'

'Oh, sweetie, that's terrible,' said Amanda. 'Poor you.'

Penny turned to her new best friend. 'I expected you to feel sympathy for the wife, and not want to know me.'

'I don't know the wife, sweetie but you seem to have paid a big price for what happened, especially if it cost you your marriage.'

'Exactly,' said Penny. 'Paul had affairs but Kaitlyn hasn't punished him. I'm not in contact with my daughter and only keep in touch with Paul through our solicitors.'

'So you've had to give up your marriage, lifestyle, family and friends. And you and your daughter aren't speaking? I don't think you should give up netball too, Penny. Why don't you have a word with Suzanne?'

'It's too late. I saw her whispering to Melanie and anyway, there's no point appealing to her good side as she doesn't have one.'

They were quiet for a moment then Penny added. 'I wouldn't mind but she wasn't even there when it happened. I was just leaving and she turned up after disappearing for months and she looked really rough. Tired and much fatter than she is now.'

'Hmm,' Amanda pressed the remote control and the gates to her villa opened. She drove up the winding drive and parked up. 'In my experience people like Suzanne often have their own secrets. Do you have the resources to find out about her past? Or even to tell her that you're going to do so if she doesn't back off?'

'I could do that, but what if there's nothing?'

'You don't know if you don't try, sweetie.'

Amanda was absolutely right. As they made their way inside for a post training snack attack, Penny decided that's exactly what she would do.

*****

Suzanne had been telling the truth. Using her stage name, Suzy Storm, she'd put the past behind her. Seeing Penny at netball reminded her of her big mistake, but Penny didn't know her secrets so Suzy was able to put it to the back of her mind. She'd managed to get a gig on a ship as a backing singer and was enjoying herself. When she'd bragged to her family and friends at home, she'd exaggerated by telling them she was going to be the

126

main attraction. Cleaning toilets didn't motivate her but Suzy loved being on the stage. She knew she was meant to sing and, for the first time in her life, worked hard. She was determined to look as good as she could both on and off stage. She behaved herself and the other entertainers had made her feel welcome. They were all different and seemed to be a tight-knit group. Using the ship's gym facilities every day under the instruction of a good-looking fitness instructor, it wasn't long before she lost the weight she'd gained and was fit and healthy.

Suzy had been working on the ship for six weeks and was on the final day of her fourth ten-day cruise. During her hot stone massage in the ship's luxurious spa, she recalled how her luck had changed before the current cruise started.

Kai, the Entertainment's Manager and himself a former performer, had approached Suzy and two of the other backing singers. Suzy recalled his conversation, which had changed everything.

'Paula's gone down with a throat infection. I need someone to replace her.'

'I'm your woman,' Bonny had said.

The others had either raised their eyebrows or looked down. Bonny was a Barbie lookalike. Unfortunately her looks were better than her voice. Kai employed her as a dancer and only used her as a backing singer in emergencies.

'Thanks for the offer, Bonny but I need your talent in the dance troupe.'

'Just trying to help, Kai,' she'd stroked her long hair. 'If there's anything else I can do...' A few of them smirked. Kai had already sailed that ship and had no intention of returning.

'Got it,' he'd said, and quickly moved on. 'So, Suzy, Di, Marie. Interested?'

They'd whooped and nodded their enthusiasm.

'Okay. You know the songs. I'll audition each of you separately and all you have to do is give it your best shot. Di. You first, then Marie and Suzy. Everyone else take a break and I'll see you back here in an hour.'

Kai had allowed the girls to watch each other. Suzy knew her voice was better than the others but she'd still had to perfect her stage presence. She preferred country songs but gave it her all singing the Tina Turner classic, Simply the Best. They'd all

127

applauded. She'd guessed the girls were just being polite, as she had been after their performances. Suzy was the only one who'd been genuinely surprised when Kai had given her the good news.

Then during her final performance as main singer the previous night, Kai had allowed her to do a set of country songs. The owner of the popular and famous *Black Knight* club had been enjoying a break on the cruise and assumed Kai was her agent. He'd approached him and asked if she would perform in his club. He was so impressed that he wanted to book her for the following night.

The treatment finished, Suzy gave a satisfied sigh and returned to the present. Feeling relaxed she dressed and made her way upstairs and outside to watch the activity. The staff and passengers waited for the pilot to take the ship into dock and as she looked over the railings as the approaching boat became larger, Suzy heard footsteps.

'Hi,' said Kai before giving her a quick kiss on the lips.

Singing wasn't the only part of her life that was going well.

*****

Suzanne hadn't been at training the following week, or for a number of weeks after, and Penny started to enjoy herself. Nobody was pointing at her or sniggering so she relaxed and got to know the other players. She now felt settled into the Expat lifestyle. They played a match on the Wednesday night and won by a margin. Melanie had played Centre and worked well with Amanda and Penny, feeding good balls into both shooters. She was a diva but an excellent player too and Penny liked her. She saw herself on a different social spectrum to Melanie so didn't plan to be friends outside the netball club.

On the Friday night following the match, she was getting ready for the country night at the *Black Knight* club. Penny left the villa and was on the pathway heading to Amanda's within a few minutes. Both villas were in an exclusive area but only a pleasant ten-minute walk to the nearest town, which was full of bars and restaurants. The famous club was on the near side of the town. The sun left a spectacular array of pinks and oranges in the sky as it started to dip below the horizon. Penny took no notice of her beautiful surroundings as she wondered what possessed her to think she should walk in her high heels. She returned home, put

128

on a pair of flatties and grabbed a bag for her heels. She called for Amanda and listened to her chatter on the relaxing walk, along the pathway adjacent to the beach. Penny was looking forward to spending the night with Amanda and a few of her friends who she hadn't yet met. Country music wasn't her favourite but Amanda said her friends had raved about the act so Penny was curious to see Suzy Storm for herself.

She hadn't made the connection.

*****

She was always nervous before a performance but tonight more so than usual. Suzy knew this was make or break. They'd already been told the audience reaction would determine any repeat bookings at the club. She gulped a swig of her vodka diet Coke, closed her eyes and took one final deep breath as the comedian warming up the audience announced her name. Suzy sauntered onto the stage and burst into song. Kai had been spot on with her opening number. As she finished singing *9 to 5* the audience applauded rapturously. Her nerves now settled, the first set flew by as Suzy interacted with the audience and enjoyed herself. They called for more as she brought the first part of her act to a close with *Jolene.*

The audience loved her and except for Penny, clapped loudly and shouted for more as she left the stage.

'I know you don't like her but the girl can sing,' said Amanda.

'I honestly didn't expect to see her here, and you're right on both counts.'

'Don't let it spoil your night, sweetie. I'll order more champers.' The waiters were rushed off their feet and despite raising her arm and clicking her fingers, they failed to materialise at the table.

'Shit. That's their tip halved,' Amanda got up. 'I'll try not to be too long.'

Amanda's other two friends were chatting to each other so Penny looked around. Suzy was standing to the side of the stage with a good-looking man who had a protective arm around her waist. It was obvious they were together. Penny wanted to throw up as she watched them being lovey dovey with each other. They turned professional as an important looking man approached and struck up a conversation. Penny looked elsewhere as she finished her drink. When she looked at them again, they were

129

heading towards the stage side door. Suzy leaned towards her man and it looked to Penny as if she whispered something to him. They both turned and looked directly at her. Penny averted her gaze as she heard them laugh, and knew that Suzy had shared the tale of her humiliation at the netball tournament.

She jumped when she heard Amanda's voice. 'Jesus, Penny what's wrong? You've gone bright red. Are you okay?'

She most definitely was not okay and decided to act on Amanda's advice.

'I'll tell you later.'

Amanda handed her a glass brimming with champagne. As she gulped it down she added Suzy Storm to her growing list of people she intended to pay back. Big time.

*****

Suzy's first proper gig ashore had been a resounding success and she was on a high. To round it off, the best-looking man she'd ever been out with was lying in the bed next to her. He certainly knew how to treat a lady, though her actions during the last half-hour hadn't been very ladylike. She giggled and Kai opened his eyes.

'What's the joke?'

'No joke. I'm just really happy for the first time in ages.'

'Me too, Suzy. Come here.'

He pulled her to him and smiled up at her before nibbling on her breast. Suzy groaned. This time she laid back and let Kai do all the work. They had two days off before another gig at the club and she intended to make the most of it.

*****

Penny knew exactly who to call. She'd employed him to dig up dirt on Paul. She wanted any information on Suzanne that she could use to humiliate or destroy the bitch. She wasn't bothered about waking him during the early hours of the morning, and Derek answered on the third ring.

'So this girl has annoyed you and you want payback?'

'It goes a little deeper than that, Derek. But yes, that's the gist of it. She disappeared for some months a while back so it would be good to know what she was up to...'

'And this couldn't wait until the morning?'

'Do you want my business or not?'

'Of course,' he made a mental note to raise his fee then putting his dislike of Penny aside, he got to work. Derek listened carefully and wrote notes where required. He was about to tell her how much money he'd need when she interrupted.

'I have another job for you.'

'Go ahead.'

'My daughter Kaitlyn attends Surrey University. I want to know every aspect of her life, specifically what she does during her down time and whether she is actually studying and working.'

'I suppose you have your reasons for not speaking to her directly?'

Penny heard the sarcasm in his voice. 'Damn right I do. Just do the job, Derek and get me any dirt you can on her, there's a good chap.'

'Will do, Penny.' *Good chap indeed. His fee went up again.*

Sucking in a breath when he told her how much, she didn't argue and arranged to transfer the funds. They hung up. Penny smiled to herself, convinced it was only a matter of time before she'd be able to humiliate both her daughter and Suzanne. She didn't have any champagne in the fridge. Making a mental note to speak to Sophia, she decided to give her another chance, but would replace her if she didn't up her game. She sighed then opened a bottle of Prosecco, it would do. Nobody messed with Penny Forbes and got away with it.

*****

He sat quietly and thought for a moment after hanging up the phone. She was such a bitch. He was going to enjoy taking her money and adding a little on the invoice to make up for her attitude. Derek had heard rumours about why she'd left England, and wondered if it was worth checking. There was nothing stopping him from investigating her. Even if nobody was paying him he might be able to earn a decent sum if the story was good enough.

Initial enquiries led to Penny's netball team. Knowing he would stand out like a sore thumb if he visited the club without a legitimate reason, he did some Internet research. The club advertised for new players and Derek made a note of the name and telephone number of the woman in charge. He phoned Rose to arrange a meeting. He didn't expect to get much information, as he knew how close women could be, but it was worth a try.

Derek got a lot more than he'd anticipated.

131

Rose wasn't what Derek had expected. Mid forties at least, she was tall and slim with short brown hair. She reminded him of the no nonsense women who took his sister guiding as a youngster. He laid his cards on the table straight away.

'Penny Forbes hired me to investigate two of your players.'

Rose gave an enquiring look. 'You mean Penny Mason?'

'She calls herself Forbes now and wants information on a girl called Suzanne, and Penny's own daughter Kaitlyn.'

'Kaitlyn? Why would she want to investigate her own daughter?'

'Perhaps we could discuss that as part of exchanging information?

'What's in it for me?'

'If the information is of use to me, I might be able to offer some monetary compensation for your time.' Sod it, thought Derek. Playboy Penny could afford it.

Rose thought for a moment. Although netball was more important than gossip, that didn't stop her from listening to private conversations whenever the opportunity arose. It was a good way to find out if they were bitching about her tactics and team choices. But as the girls were more concerned with their private lives than the beautiful game, she would often overhear stories that shocked her. She didn't know much about Kaitlyn and Suzanne, but it was a different story with the others. Rose made it her business to know theirs. She looked at the vetting forms of those who worked for her, knowing that the buck stopped with her if any of the girls employed turned out to be security risks. Carol's in particular had made interesting reading, and if she had not been worried that her discovery might have caused opposing teams to object to Carol playing in a ladies team, she would have been tempted to spread that bit of gossip. Knowing that revealing information she had obtained from vetting forms could drop her in hot water, she always kept a lid on her findings. Knowledge was power after all.

'I know everything that goes on at that club. The girls can't even focus on netball for a few hours a week without allowing their private lives to take over.' Rose tutted and shook her head. 'That said I don't know much about Kaitlyn. Plays her cards close to her chest that one. I do know that she recently changed universities so you might want to check that out. As for

132

Suzanne, she's a nasty piece of work but I haven't seen her for a while. She disappeared for a few months, came back fatter and feistier but didn't hang around. I got the feeling she was running from something. Maybe if you found out where she was, you'd get some answers?' Now Rose was opening up she couldn't resist spilling the beans on the rest of her ungrateful team-mates. Derek assured her that none of the information she provided would lead back to her, so she got it all off her chest.

Trying to hide his surprise he made the deal then made notes on each player. If he thought Penny was a bitch, this woman was definitely top dog. With every new revelation Rose revealed, Derek saw pound signs. Written correctly this could be one hell of a tabloid story. He'd often investigated on behalf of the *Sunday Sensation,* and he knew a particularly grubby little reporter that would pay good money for a sordid tale such as this.

*****

The second time in the club was even better than the first. It was almost Christmas and the place was heaving. Kai was standing at the bar watching the audience as Suzy gave it her all. He wondered about the man at the large table in front of the stage. His companions were enjoying themselves but he seemed to be studying Suzy intently. Kai didn't have to wait long as he watched the man lean over and speak to another man at the table. They both looked towards Kai and the messenger left the table and approached the bar.

'Hi. I'm Dave Knox. I work for Mr Carter,' he nodded towards his boss. 'Mr Carter asked if you'd be kind enough to join us.'

They made their way to the table and Dave did the introductions.

'So, Kai, you're Suzy's agent right?'

Kai explained he was indeed her agent and partner.

'My company's about to produce a TV show in the UK. *Stand By Your Star* will start in the New Year and we aim to find the next big UK Country Star, voted for by the people of Britain. Suzy would be perfect for the show. Think she'd be interested?'

'I'll have a word.' Kai played it cool but knew this would be the making of her.

*****

The party season came and went and Suzy was busy singing and recording for the show. Her attendance at netball had

133

dwindled. She knew Kai wanted her to quit the sport to concentrate on her singing, but she still enjoyed having a laugh with the girls and winding-up posh Penny. It was also a good way to stay fit and a welcome change from the gym work.

Penny's face dropped when she saw her in January, but decided to ignore her. Suzy was having none of it. Penny felt on edge and glanced in Suzy's direction throughout the session, like an animal knowing it was going to the abbatoir. As they came off the court for a drink after the drills, Suzy slowed down and whispered to Penny.

'Shagged anyone else's husband lately? They all know what you're like you know.'

Something snapped. She grabbed Suzy by the arm but smiled at the others. 'Can I have a word?'

Suzy hesitated, about to tell her where to go when she saw the look in her eyes. The others were watching so Penny let go of Suzy but headed for the door. Without looking back she knew she was following. Outside she walked around the corner of the building where they wouldn't be heard.

'Who have you told?'

'That's for me to know and you to...'§

'Stop it you stupid little bitch!'

Suzy was taken aback. Her bravado disappeared and for the first time, she was frightened of Penny. She made a move but Penny grabbed her arm and squeezed tightly.

'Ow. Geroff, you're hurting me. I haven't said anything, honest.'

'I saw you talking to Melanie about me, and to your boyfriend. Who else knows?'

'Nobody, honest. I was just winding you up.' Suzy crossed her fingers behind her back. The damage was already done, but she wasn't to know that.

Penny didn't believe her. 'I'm not the only one with a past, am I, Suzanne?' she said her name with venom. Suzy paled.

'If you ruin my reputation here I'll pay you back tenfold. Do you understand?'

She said she did so Penny let go of her arm. As Suzy ran away from her, Penny wondered whether the girl's terrified look was because she had something to hide or because Penny had frightened her. She wouldn't have long to wait to find out.

*****

134

Derek and his reporter friend had worked hard on his investigation. They followed some of the leads from Rose and their gut instinct at other times. The icing on the cake was discovering that Suzanne was now Suzy Storm. That put their story in a different league and their reward for their efforts from the tabloid, and the exorbitant fee Derek would extract from Penny, would put him into a different tax bracket. Rose would receive a generous payment, but first he needed to finish his business with Penny.

*****

A package arrived for Penny the following day, special delivery. Her phone rang as she was about to open it.

'Yes,' she answered.

'It's Derek. I have news.'

'I'm listening.'

'You'll no doubt be pleased to know that your daughter is knuckling down with her studies and is a model student. In fact, she goes home most weekends and it appears your husband is training her for some sort of role within his business empire.'

She wasn't pleased. 'Anything else?'

Her attitude sucked and he disliked her, but Derek knew Penny would be pleased with what he'd discovered. He was a little reluctant to share his discovery with her, but wanted to fleece the bitch for her money so knew he'd have to give her something to justify the large invoice she was about to receive. He didn't tell her that he also had plans to use the information.

'Oh, yes. About the girl.'

Her mood changed significantly as she listened to the news. Her gut instinct had been right and she had the information she needed to ruin Suzanne's reputation. Very satisfied she thanked Derek and hung up.

Now for the package. She opened the official-looking brown envelope, read and re-read the letter. So Paul was willing to give her half of everything as long as she kept her mouth shut about Kaitlyn. The prostitution was enough to humiliate Kaitlyn and ruin her reputation, but Derek had confirmed that she was now behaving herself. It only took a moment for Penny to make her decision. The money and assets were always going to win. She signed the forms agreeing to Paul's terms. It didn't occur to her that her estranged husband and daughter had something far more precious than any amount of money could buy.

135

Chapter 15

Daniel was sleeping peacefully during one of his twice weekly visits, while Ann and Marsha made themselves comfortable in front of the TV. The DNA test had proved Ann was his grandmother and she'd applied to adopt him. The application process was long-winded but she'd been given visiting rights in the meantime. The authorities hadn't found his birth mother.

Ann and Marsha were looking forward to the new series *Stand By Your Star,* especially as the lush country singer Chuck Allbright, was one of the judges. Colin was looking after his grandchildren that weekend so it was a night in front of the telly for the ladies, without him.

Marsha broke a chunk of chocolate off the bar and took a slurp of tea before popping the chocolate into her mouth. She closed her eyes and savoured the sweet creamy taste, melted by the hot liquid. Ann smiled.

'Open your eyes or you're going to miss the start.'

The credits rolled and the judges were revealed. They knew all about Chuck but were keen to see which unqualified Z-listers had been plucked from obscurity to judge the latest vehicle to get the general public spending their money on voting.

'Oh look,' said Marsha. 'It's wassername. The one who was in that band then went solo. Used to be married to...'

'Oh I know,' said Ann. 'Married to that fella before he turned gay. What's his name now?'

Marsha didn't want to get into the whole *turning gay* discussion with her mother-in-law, who she thought had some strange ideas on the subject. Instead they discussed the identity of the three lesser-known judges while waiting to see the acts.

The presenter was the famous – infamous to some – Dandy Vickers. He was always in the headlines for his inappropriate comments or extra-marital affairs. *His long-suffering wife must be an angel* thought Marsha as he walked onto the stage to rapturous applause. He welcomed the audience then introduced the judges. A montage of their most memorable moments followed and the cameras panned to each one, as they tried without success to look modest.

'C'mon, get on with it,' Ann shouted at the TV and Marsha shushed her.

137

'You'll wake him if you keep that up.'

'Sorry,' she said. They looked at each other, communicating silently.

'Do you want to take him up or shall I?' Ann asked and Marsha said she'd do it. The show went to a break and she gathered Daniel in her arms. Ann gave him a kiss on the cheek and he stirred but didn't wake.

'I'll get us some more snacks while you put him down.'

As she returned downstairs, the show had come back on and was about to get underway.

'Our first act is originally from Bloomington but now she spends her time between working on a cruise ship in the Med, or a top club in Spain,' said Dandy Vickers.

'Ooh, I wonder if we know her,' Ann joked. The area was sprawling and besides for the countryside, was highly populated. Marsha gave her an *as if* look.

'There's already a whole lot of talk about this girl, but let's see what you, the audience think. Ladies and Gentlemen, I give you Suzy Storm.'

The audience were already warmed up and clapped as if Elvis had appeared on stage. Life then seemed to go into slow motion in Ann's house. Despite Suzy Storm's Dolly Parton-esque get up, she recognised the girl straight away.

Ann paled then looked at the place on the settee where Daniel had been lying minutes before. Then she looked at Marsha who was watching her mother-in-law's reaction intently. The initial look of confusion on Marsha's face turned to one of recognition. She looked back to the screen and recognised Suzanne.

'I don't believe...' Marsha took a breath. 'Really, Ann?' But she already knew the answer.

'You know her?'

'I worked with her and played netball with her too. When I was starting out she made my life hell,' she tried to control her emotions. 'I thought it was because I was a newbie. But it all makes sense now.'

'Marsha, I'm so sorry. I didn't know.'

'So she's Daniel's mother.' It wasn't a question. 'She had an affair with Keith, had a baby then swanned off after leaving him with you and you didn't think to tell me?'

138

'But it wasn't like that! How was I supposed to know that you two knew each other? Obviously I would have...'

'Would have what, Ann?'

'Would have told you of course.'

They both stopped talking as Suzy's sweet voice reached them. 'When we worked together I always wondered how she could sound like an angel but be such a bitch. I'm going to make her pay for this.'

Ann wanted to say something but the look on Marsha's face stopped her. Both were unaware that somebody else was already planning to make Suzanne pay, big style.

*****

The show was being broadcast live in Spain via Expat TV. Penny was already aware that Suzy Storm was one of the acts, and had discussed her plan with Amanda.

'You know if this information goes public it will ruin her career and her relationship? Are you sure you want to do this? Absolutely certain?' asked Amanda.

'Can I remind you that it was you who suggested it? And I'm only telling the owner of the club and her boyfriend, it's not like I'm broadcasting it around the world...I'll let others do that.'

'Of course,' Amanda took a sip of her drink and gave a satisfied smile. 'But I didn't expect you to be quite so vindictive.'

'As they say, Amanda. Hell hath no fury...'

She made a mental note never to cross her new best friend. 'But what if she retaliates? Have you thought about that?'

'She couldn't do any worse than my daughter already has. People know that I enjoy the company of younger men and so what. I'm a free agent now and not hurting anyone.'

It was a fair point. They'd arranged a pampering session the following day at the five star resort along the coast. Later in the evening Amanda was hosting a party for a number of her single, and a few attached friends. The male guests were all young, fit and short of money so the arrangement suited them all.

Bella had left some canapés so they settled down with their drinks and nibbles looking forward to watching the show. Penny still thought of Suzy Storm as Suzanne, and was looking forward to seeing her being knocked off her pedestal.

*****

Suzy knew she had a good voice, but was totally unprepared for the public's reaction. She lost her cockiness on

139

camera and appeared genuinely shy. The camera loved her and so did the audience, both in the studio and the viewers at home. As she left the studio after her last performance in week three, there was a queue of fans vying for her autograph. Kai was thrilled with the news she was now the bookies' favourite.

The next morning the story broke.

The papers were delivered to their hotel room and Kai's jaw dropped when he saw the photograph on the front page of the *Sunday Sensation*. The headline from two weeks before had been *Suzy Causes a Storm*. The current headline wasn't only about Suzy. *It's Not all Flowers in Bloomington* it read with the sub-heading *Bloomington Netball Scandal*. There were a few photographs. Kai knew that CCTV systems were a sign of the times in cities and towns these days. He was amazed that a reporter had been able to find the exact still of Suzy in a city as big as Skeltingham. How could they do that? Suzy's face was clear enough to recognise and she was obviously carrying a bundle containing a baby. The second photograph was one of the posh bird Kai had met in the club in Spain. She was draped across a bed naked with what looked like a post-sex smile on her face. The paper had blacked out the intimate parts of her body with pictures of flowers.

The accompanying article listed six of the players, giving basic details of their particular scandal. It had all been a covert investigation. The reporter hadn't interviewed any of the women but had spoken briefly to Suzy Storm's sister. The article concluded by saying that, when asked if she knew she was an aunt, Suzy's sister had replied. *'O.M.G! Seriously?!'*

It was compelling reading. For some reason the report showed the main position each played, followed by the scandal related to them.

Suzy – Wing Attack. Had an affair and a secret baby by the husband of one of the other players.

Marsha – Goal Keeper. Had a child of her own aged just fourteen after being raped by her alcoholic mother's then boyfriend. She was forced to give up the baby – the only blood relative she now has. Her husband tragically died and she came home one day to discover that a baby had been abandoned on her mother-in-law's doorstep. The baby's mother we now know is Suzy Storm.

140

Carol – Goal Attack. Used to be a man called Mark. Acrimonious divorce from her previous wife and was estranged from her children. Her two sons who are now adults want to re-establish contact.

Penny – Goal Shooter. Is a delight. Especially if you are an exotic young man in need of a quick thrill and a free dinner. Penny's ex, the entrepreneur Paul Mason, is currently divorcing his wife.

Kaitlyn – Goal Defence. Poor little rich girl and Penthouse Penny's unfortunate daughter. As if her mother's antics weren't embarrassing enough her father, the entrepreneur Paul Mason paid another man to have an affair and photograph his soon to be ex wife to ensure a quick divorce.

Sandy – Wing Defence. is now licking her wounds in Fiji after discovering it was her husband who had a passionate affair with Penny.

'Fucking shit!' Kai banged his forehead with a fist.

'What's up?' Suzy heard him shout and the paper rustle. She rolled over in bed, stretched and yawned. 'Come here my handsome tiger.' She sat up in bed letting the sheet roll off her to reveal her breasts.

'Not now, Suzy.'

It was the first time he hadn't fallen for her charms, and she knew something was wrong. She put on a t-shirt and got out of bed. 'What is it, Kai?' she could see he was reading the paper. 'Didn't they like it?' Everyone seemed to enjoy her singing so she was genuinely surprised.

'It's nothing to do with your singing. Why didn't you tell me?'

She knew without looking at the paper, but she read it anyway. 'Jesus Christ! Carol used to be a man and Kaitlyn's Dad paid Leon to sleep with Penny. Oh my God. Marsha had a kid when she was just fourteen?'

'Never mind bloody Carol, Kaitlyn and Marsha,' Kai shook his head. 'For fuck's sake, Suzy. You didn't think to tell me that you had a baby, then abandoned him on some woman's doorstep?'

She knew she was in trouble and her whole attitude changed. 'I'm so sorry, Kai. I was ashamed and suffering with depression. I loved his dad but felt so alone when he died. There was no one I could turn to and I didn't know what to do. And it

141

wasn't just *some woman*. It was the baby's grandmother.' She started crying. Kai held her, his mind racing with thoughts of how they could limit the damage. Suzy seemed genuinely upset. He was still annoyed but it didn't stop him from loving her or sympathising with the situation she'd been in.

'What about your family? Why didn't you ask for their help?'

'They would have been ashamed of the mess I'd got myself into. It was Marsha's husband and I worked and played netball with her. How could I tell everyone I was having her dead husband's baby?'

He was beginning to understand her predicament so started to calm down. He needed some space.

'I'm going out. I need to think.'

'Don't leave me, Kai,' she begged and wrapped her arms around his waist, hugging as tightly as she could.

'I'm not leaving you. I need to clear my head and think about our next move. It could be the end of your dream, Suzy and neither of us want that.'

She loosened her grip, and nodded her understanding.

'I need to speak to my parents. My mother's not going to be very happy.'

Kai had no idea whether Suzy's Mum already knew she was a grandmother, or if she had found out by reading the newspaper. Either way, he thought *not going to be very happy* was a gross understatement.

'Phone your parents but make it quick. Arrange for them to come to the hotel as soon as they can. But don't answer the phone or the door while I'm out, just in case it's one of those flaming reporters. Understand?'

As Kai reached the foyer he saw reporters and cameramen camping outside the hotel. 'Shit,' he muttered to himself. Before anyone outside saw him he moved to the back of the lobby and ran down the emergency exit, heading for the gymnasium. He would have to use the treadmill instead of pounding the streets. By the time his workout had finished he'd planned their response and hoped the public would be sympathetic to Suzy Storm's plight.

*****

142

Ann and Marsha were upstairs getting Daniel ready to return to his Foster family when they heard a lot of noise coming from outside.

'Sounds like a proper kerfuckle,' said Ann.

'I think you mean kerfuffle,' Marsha replied.

'I know what I mean. Put Daniel in the pram while I go and see what's happening.'

Holding the baby, Marsha followed Ann downstairs and headed for the living room while Ann went to investigate. She was almost blinded by the flashlights as she opened the front door, then came to her senses quickly and closed it.

'Marsha, Marsha.'

'What is it?' she looked up from tucking Daniel in.

'A crowd of photographers and reporters outside in the street, that's what.'

'Where, Ann? Has there been an accident or something? What's happened?'

'Right outside here, on the pavement. One of the cheeky sods took a photo of me.'

'What's going on?'

The phone rang as somebody knocked at the door. Ann headed towards the door but Marsha called to her as she went to answer the phone. 'Don't answer it, Ann.' Her mother-in-law did as bid. Marsha answered the phone. It was Carol, in tears.

'Marsha don't speak to anyone and don't answer the door until you've read it.'

'Read what? What the hell is going on?'

'It's the *Sunday Sensation*. They've done a piece about a so called scandal in our netball team. Six of us have been targeted and it's not good news.' Carol gave her the gist of the story, stumbling through the part about Marsha's rape and crying when speaking about her own mention in the cruel article. 'You're not going to be able to get to the shop to get yourself a copy, but I'll email you a link to the website.'

'Okay, what do I do?'

Carol had forgotten what a Luddite Marsha was. 'Fire up your computer and open the new email from me. The text that is in blue and underlined is the link. Click on it with your mouse and it'll take you to the online version of the article.'

'Will do.' She was about to hang up then realised she hadn't asked her friend how she was. 'It's out there now, Marsha. Nothing I can do about it.'

'And what about Sam, and your sons?'

'Sam is absolutely furious but is going to stand by me, as you said he would if I talked to him.'

Marsha was glad to be proved right. 'And your boys?'

'Callum phoned to say that nothing changes for him and Brent, they still want to see me.'

'Oh thank God for that,' said Marsha.

'I almost forgot to tell you what with everything else that's going on. Suzy Storm's boyfriend phoned. No idea how he got my number but I don't care at this stage. He wants to help us so we all come up with a united response. I hope you don't mind but I've said we'll meet him. I'll give you a chance to read the article. Call me back when you're done.'

Marsha was dumbstruck. She hung up, told Ann what had happened then went to dig their old computer out of the drawer. As she fired it up and looked for the password information, the phone rang again.

'I've got it,' said Ann.

'That was the Social Worker,' she said shortly after. 'They know all about the story in the paper and are coming round for Daniel. They're going to come across the field to the back door and hope to avoid that rabble out the front. They'll be accompanied by police who can help out if required.' She took a deep breath and shook her head. 'What are we going to do?' she asked as she leant over Marsha to read the article.

Marsha was gutted that everyone now knew her past. Even thought she hadn't done anything wrong, the horrendous memories came flooding back. Ann could see how upset she was.

'Maybe the police can find him if he's still alive, Marsha. Then he can be punished and you will have justice, at long last.'

She hadn't thought of that. 'Perhaps. It's all so sudden. I was going to say I don't want to hang my dirty washing in public, but I think it's a bit late for that. Let's get Daniel to safety first, then we can think about what we want to do.'

'Fair enough, but I'm with you all the way, whatever you decide.'

Marsha smiled her thanks.

144

Police had moved the few media people from the back of Ann's property. One had been arrested for trespassing when they caught him rifling through her rubbish. After saying goodbye to Daniel, Ann asked when she'd be able to see him again. The Social Worker was vague.

'I'll make arrangements to meet so we can discuss future visits.'

'But can't we arrange a date now?' Ann chewed at a fingernail after asking the question.

'I'm sure you understand, Mrs Lawson, that we have to find out whether Suzy Storm is actually Daniel's mother. The police will want to interview you about that.'

'She is his mother. I saw her on the TV last night and in the paper this morning. I assumed the police wouldn't want to deal with it during the weekend so was going to call with the details on Monday.'

Nice one Ann, thought Marsha. The Social Worker wasn't to know they'd seen the series from the start.

'I'm sure you were,' the Social Worker replied with insincerity. 'But we have to follow procedures.'

'But I'm his grandmother!'

'Mrs Lawson, please understand that we all have Daniel's best interests at heart. I'll phone you as soon as I can. Okay?'

Ann calmed down. She trusted the woman who had been extremely helpful throughout the whole process. It was unfair to take her frustration out on her. 'Okay, thanks. I'm sorry it's just...'

'I know it can't be easy for you but I also know you adore Daniel and I'll do everything in my power... I'll leave it at that and I'll be in touch.'

They left the same way they arrived.

Marsha called Carol and explained the delay.

'Right. I hope you haven't made any arrangements because you, me, Kaitlyn and her father are meeting with Suzy and her bloke this afternoon.'

'What!? If you think I'm going to be in the same room as that deceiving effing slapper, you've got another think coming. I'll throttle the bloody...'

Carol resisted the urge to tell Marsha off for swearing. It was more than understandable under the circumstances.

145

'Perhaps you and Suzanne should have a chat first, in private?'

'I think that's a good idea, Carol. Ann will be there as well this afternoon. She's as involved in all this as any of us.'

*****

Suzy lay on the bed in her jeans and jumper, nervously awaiting the arrival of her parents and Chardonnay. For Kai's plan to work, she had to get them on side.

Kai stopped her from biting her nails as they waited. She jumped when she heard a rap on the door, then got up from the bed and went to open it.

'I'm so sorry.' She burst into tears and threw herself at her mother, hugging with all her might. Her mother's arms remained at her side, initially, but after a few seconds she couldn't help herself.

'There, there, baby. That's right. You let it all out, Suzanne. Everything's going to be all right.'

Chardonnay watched as her mother stroked her sister's hair. Suzanne could always worm her way around her mother but even Chardonnay found it hard to believe that her sister was going to get off so lightly. Suzanne looked at her, then at her father. She stopped sobbing and stepped out of the embrace.

'I'm sorry, Mum. I really am.' She turned to her father. 'Can I have a hug please?'

Mike was upset and annoyed at what she'd done, but that didn't stop him from loving her. He opened his arms and they embraced.

And the Oscar goes to... thought Chardonnay as she watched her sister's latest performance.

After letting go of her father, Suzy turned to her sister. 'Chardonnay?'

No way Jose, she thought as she folded her arms, but her mother didn't give her much choice.

'Your sister's been through a lot, Chardonnay. Give her a hug.'

'But...'

Her father turned his head and whispered. 'Go on, love. We want to make sure we can see our grandson. Do it for me and your Mum. Then we'll all sit down and get to the bottom of this.'

Chardonnay let her sister hug her, and returned the embrace with as little enthusiasm as she could get away with.

146

Kai coughed to remind them of his presence and the introductions were made.

'Kai helped me get through post-natal depression and the shame of what I'd done. He also convinced me to tell you everything and has arranged therapy sessions.'

Suzy told the story exactly as Kai had instructed and her parents swallowed every line. Grateful to be given an excuse to forgive their daughter, Kai could see Suzy's sister looked doubtful, but that didn't matter. The parents would want to see their grandchild so would make Chardonnay behave.

'Tell me everything,' said Hazel.

'I don't want to go through it all again, Mum, it's too painful.'

'Suzanne. We are your family and we need to know what's happened to make you do this.'

They sat down and Suzanne explained she'd met Keith at work. 'He was having problems at home. His wife was horrible to him.'

'But Marsha's lovely,' said Chardonnay.

'She might well be,' snapped Suzy. 'But not in the bedroom.'

Chardonnay had heard enough. 'Is there a kettle?'

'Yes but I'll call for room service,' said Kai.

'It's okay. I'll go to reception and order if you like? Tea, coffee and sandwiches?' Chardonnay needed to get out before she opened her mouth and ruined their little reunion.

Her father said that would be fine. 'Perhaps when I return you could let me know when I'll be able to see my nephew, Suzanne?'

'No need to take that attitude. If you knew what I'd been through maybe you wouldn't be so...'

'We all want to see him, Chardonnay,' said Mike. 'Isn't that right, love?' he added, looking towards his wife.

'Your sister is right, Suzanne. When can we see him? What's his name and how old is he?'

She didn't tell them that Ann had named her baby and she'd only discovered his name that morning.

'It's Daniel, and he's almost five months old. We'll make the arrangements when Ann, his other grandmother arrives for the meeting.'

Chardonnay made her way to the door as she heard Kai outlining his plan. The other netball girls were also coming to the meeting. Chardonnay smiled at the thought. How would Marsha react when she saw Suzanne? Would Carol look any different now they knew she was once a man? And would Kaitlyn be so superior now everyone knew her mother was a tart and her father a home wrecker?

She didn't have to wait long to find out.

*****

As she arrived at the hotel with Ann and they made their way up to the suite, Marsha knew that being in the same room as Suzanne was going to be difficult. She'd underestimated her emotions. Kaitlyn and a man Marsha presumed to be her father were already there, so were Carol and Suzanne's boyfriend. Despite everything that had happened, Suzanne stood there looking smug and Marsha lost it. She was across the room in a second, her body seemingly moving on autopilot. She had Suzanne by the throat and forced her into the wall.

'You evil bitch!'

Suzanne's look of smugness turned to one of terror and shock. The red mist left as quickly as it had arrived. She let go before anyone had a chance to pull her off. Suzanne milked it and cowered against the wall.

'She's mad, no wonder her husband...' Suzy thought better of it, deciding not to pursue a verbal fight. Even though it went against all her natural instincts, Kai had told her to behave and she needed him on side.

'I think we should all calm down,' said Kai.

'Calm down,' said Carol. 'A national newspaper wants to ruin my life, the media have been hounding me all morning and my husband was close to leaving me. If that's not enough, your vicious girlfriend thinks it's acceptable to treat my best friend like shit, dump her new born baby, and you want us to calm down!'

'I don't feel very calm either,' said Kaitlyn. 'How can I go back to uni now everyone knows about Mummy, and Daddy's going to be a laughing stock.

Marsha looked around the room. They were all emotional cripples and the situation seemed farcical. Her lips twitched. If somebody told her a story like theirs, she wouldn't believe it in a million years. Ann noticed Marsha's amusement and so did Carol. Ann coughed, trying to hide her own chuckles,

Carol wasn't as successful. The initial amazement of the others turned to mirth and soon they were all laughing. The hotel staff arrived with afternoon tea. They'd been warned to expect a sombre atmosphere given the paper's revelations, but couldn't wait to leave the room, assuming the occupants were nutters or had been taking illegal substances.

Once the manic laughter had subsided, Kai started to unveil his plan to turn a negative into a positive. Paul knew the situation could have been worse. If they'd found Evie he was grateful she'd kept her mouth shut and Kaitlyn's unsavoury job hadn't been exposed. Although initially sceptical, Paul soon saw a window of opportunity to ensure he and his daughter were perceived as victims. If he played this right it would be great publicity for his business. Now enthused, Paul and Kai became a tag team, bouncing ideas off each other. They came up with a joint plan and although it sounded good to the ladies, Marsha felt compelled to point out the flaw.

'Trouble is the Weakest Link,' she nodded towards Suzanne. 'It involves her being sorry for everything and I don't see any of that.'

Suzy's feelings towards Marsha hadn't changed, but Kai had left her in no doubt of the consequences if she didn't behave herself and agree to the plan. She wanted fame and Kai in equal measure so was well motivated. Still upset after having to explain everything to her family, she tried to hide her feelings as she always did, by putting up emotional barriers so others couldn't get close. Chardonnay knew exactly what she was like but others didn't.

'I am sorry,' said Suzy. 'I was terrified after Keith died and too ashamed to tell my family I was pregnant, and that the baby's father wasn't only dead, but had left a widow. Can you image how lonely I felt?'

My heart bleeds, thought Marsha. As Suzanne carried on with her tale of woe, Marsha watched the reaction of the others. Everyone believed her. *If she can put on this performance for us, there's a chance the public might actually believe her too.* Marsha zoned out until Kaitlyn's father spoke.

'So. Do we all agree that Suzy tells her story and the rest of us keep our mouths shut, for the time being that is?'

149

The others didn't have a problem with the plan, having no desire to speak to any members of the media. They left feeling more in control than when they'd arrived.

*****

After reading the article, the public turned against Suzy Storm. They were like a pack of wild dogs and there was a frenzy of posts on Social Media, vilifying her for abandoning her baby. *Stand By Your Star* made an announcement that she was to be dropped.

Suzy's story in the rival paper *Streetwise* the following Sunday changed everything. In what they called an open and honest interview, Suzy talked about her depression following the death of her lover, her guilt at falling for a married man, and the shame she'd brought on her family and friends. She also publicly thanked her family and netball buddies for their love and support, and apologised to Marsha. The public loved it and Suzy was reinstated into the show. Young girls with their own problems were able to relate to her and she became an unexpected role model. They voted for her in the thousands. During the following weeks the Sunday paper published the stories of the other players, except Penny who refused to cooperate. Kaitlyn and her father were happy to fill in her part of the tale. Paul also made sure that the papers learned of his generosity towards Evie; paying for her education to thank her for supporting his daughter when they'd learned of Penny's betrayal. How he intended to set Sandy up in one of his shops and finance the rest of her families' trip to join her. How he had only paid Leon to take the photographs after he had learnt of his wife's affair with the soldier. Although this was a blatant lie, Leon was prepared to confirm this for a substantial payment. He knew Sandy wasn't coming back so saw no point in cutting off his nose to spite his bank balance. Paul even managed to spin his treatment of Sayid, stating that he knew his wife had corrupted this loyal family man and had moved him to Scotland to give him and his family a fresh start. Sayid remembered Brian's warning and was happy to keep his mouth shut.

*****

It was the live final of *Stand By Your Star* and the netball girls, now mini-celebrities since publication of their story, were on the VIP guest list. The audience, some of whom had won their tickets, were being treated to a gala dinner during the performances by the six remaining finalists.

150

Marsha felt like a star as she stepped out of the limo onto the red carpet. She'd invited Ann as her plus one and the flashes from the cameras almost blinded them as they posed for photographs while waiting for the others. To everyone's relief Sam was with Carol. Sandy was back from Fiji and was busy planning for the arrival of her mother and children. She had been overwhelmed by Paul's generosity and, now she believed him to be as much a victim as she was, had grown close to the man who had helped to ruin her marriage. So much so that she had contemplated taking him as her plus one to the event. Although Kaitlyn was pleased that her father and Sandy were getting close, she was worried about her mother's reaction. Penny still knew the truth and although her father had paid her a substantial amount not to tell the truth regarding Leon, Sayid and her spell in vice, Kaitlyn knew her mother was still vying for revenge. Fortunately Sandy agreed being seen with Paul at this time might not be ideal, but as she was keen to let her ex see she was managing fine without him, she had asked Gary to accompany her. Hopefully Leon would see the footage and assume she was dating. Being a true gentleman, Gary agreed but Sandy had already nudged him twice as his eyes roamed over Marsha. She didn't really blame him. Marsha looked drop dead gorgeous in the purple ball gown that showed off her newly trim and athletic figure. They made a striking group, the fit ladies in their beautiful dresses, with their partners and the men in their smart tuxedos.

'Hey, Bloomers,' called one of the photographers. The netballers were used to their new nickname and gave the man a wave. They were asked to pose without their escorts and the girls did as requested. Everyone was enjoying themselves until a pressman decided to push his luck.

'Hey, Sam. When did you find out your Mrs was a Mr?'

The man had his pass around his neck on the official *Stand By Your Star* embossed ribbon.

'You cheeky fucker,' said Sam as he grabbed the ribbon and pulled it tight around the man's neck, cutting off his oxygen supply. The pressman struggled but Sam was much stronger. Others were taking photos but he didn't care.

'This is what happens when you disrespect my gorgeous wife. Get it?' said Sam as he loosened his grip and pushed the man away.

151

'I was only having a laugh,' the man muttered as he stroked his throat.

'Having a laugh were you, mate? Think taking the piss out of my wife is funny do you?'

Paul could see Sam was about to strike the man so he put an arm around his shoulder and steered him towards the women. Sam didn't want to spoil the night so shrugged at Carol and gave a guilty smile. Then he made a big deal of kissing her leaving no doubt as to his true feelings. Carol loved it and so did the media. The cameramen clicked away happily and the reporters were already recording the story for the gossip hungry British public.

'Thanks,' Carol whispered. 'But you'll probably get sued or arrested for assault.'

'And I'd do it all over again for my beautiful wife. You look stunning tonight.' She was walking on air as she kissed his cheek and they made their way into the building.

*****

Rose had tried to ignore the excitement at netball when they were talking about going to the show. But now as she watched the TV, she couldn't deny it. They looked fantastic and shouldn't have been there. Everything had backfired and instead of being taught a lesson by their screwed up lives, they'd been turned into mini celebrities. The money from Derek had bought her a new three-piece suite and paid for the holiday, but that was no consolation. She turned off the TV.

'Oi, I was watching that.'

'Shut up, Rory.'

'You're jealous because you snitched on them and you've made them into stars.'

'I said shut up!' Rose left the room, slamming the door behind her.

*****

At the same time in Spain, Penny turned off the TV. It wasn't fair that they were at the show. It wasn't fair that he was divorcing her and her daughter didn't want to know her and life, generally, was not fair. She hated them all! Picking up the bottle of Prosecco, she threw it at the wall.

The doorbell rang. Penny looked at the mess on the wall and floor, deciding to leave it for Sophie to deal with in the morning. She went to answer the door.

'Hi, sweetie. How are you?'

152

She smiled at Amanda. At least she had one true friend. 'I think you know the answer to that one.'

'Well I have a surprise that's bound to cheer you up. Put on your glad rags and make sure they're tight enough to show off your wonderful figure.'

'Ooh, I love surprises, especially the six foot tall olive skinned, muscled variety. Is it one of those?'

'Now that would be telling. Hurry up, sweetie. The party'll be in full swing by the time we get there.'

Penny did as bid and tingled with anticipation. It was exactly what she needed to take her mind off her problems.

Epilogue

When her name was called out Suzy couldn't believe it. The public really did love her and made her the first ever winner of the show. After the commotion of the results the studio was buzzing and it had taken a while for everyone to calm down. The music contract had already been prepared and Kai had given it the okay. Suzy was glowing as she signed it. She was going to be one of Dandy Vickers' stable of singers and was walking on air as she signed autographs for the audience members who had won their tickets. Then she made her way to her new dressing room where her family were waiting.

'Congratulations, darling,' said her father and gave her a warm kiss.

'Well done,' said Chardonnay. 'But what happens to Daniel now?'

Trust Chardonnay to put a damper on things. 'Mum and Ann are going to carry on looking after him, for now. Aren't you, Mum?'

'Of course. Well done for winning, Suzanne.' Hazel would never get over what her daughter had done but was trying her best to come to terms with it, and there was Daniel to consider. They were working with the Social Services to do whatever was best for their grandson, both grandmothers knowing that Suzanne would never look after her little boy.

'I'm thrilled,' said Suzanne. 'We're starting the tour next week so I need to see Danny before I go. Must get some photos with the press, too when I'm with him.'

'O.M.G! You are...' started Chardonnay, but her mother silenced her with a look.

She knew exactly how her youngest daughter felt. It took a will of steel not to throttle Suzanne.

*****

Marsha watched the after show shenanigans. She could see Suzy Storm signing autographs and chatting to audience members. It was only a matter of time. Suzy couldn't hide her true nature and the public couldn't be hoodwinked for long. She was a jammy cow but Marsha was certain she'd be the architect of her own downfall.

It had been a brilliant night, despite Suzanne winning. She giggled to herself hardly able to believe her own situation.

Get over yourself love she thought, knowing their stories would soon be no more than chip shop wrapping paper. She intended to make the most of it until then and looked around, locking eyes with Gary.

Marsha felt a tingle in her tummy. Perhaps it was time to move on.

Netball Quotes

I asked some friends and former team-mates what netball meant to them, and here's what they said:

"Live, love, laugh and play netball.'
Mandy Jones

"Just for me #my time #my world."
Sarah Stagg (a busy working wife and mother of three)

"There is no I in team, it's a game of seven."
Mandy Watts

"I was never too much of a fan of netball, but on a drunken night out I was persuaded to play. This was the best decision I ever made, as it has changed my life forever. It was on the court I fell in love, I met the person of my dreams and our lives together began. I don't play anymore, but I'm happy to be on the sidelines supporting the woman I love, playing the game she loves. So to netball I will be forever grateful what it has brought to my life. Thank you."
Louise Gibson

On the front of a netball team t-shirt: "Epi netballers do it..."
And on the back: "in 7 different positions!"
Episkopi Netball Team

"Netball to me is over 50 years of playing a wonderful game and making so many friends from all over the world. A school court in the West Midlands, the top of a mountain in Switzerland and military bases in Germany. Such wonderful memories."
Shirl from Verl

Acknowledgements

Thanks to my husband Allan for listening (or doing a good job of pretending to listen), to my editors Philip McAllister-Jones and Rachel Crawford (her books are awesome) and to Trudy Eitschberger, Julie Woodruff, Sarah Stagg and Mandy Jones. Thanks also to my family and all my other friends for their support.

Author's Note

Thanks for purchasing this book. I hope you enjoyed it.

If you'd like a free e-copy of the first book in my Unlikely Soldiers series, here are the links:

(Amazon) http://smarturl.it/m202d6

(Elsewhere) https://www.books2read.com/u/b6Q71p

Connect with me at: https://debmcewansbooksandblogs.com or: https://www.facebook.com/DebMcEwansbooksandblogs/?ref=bookmarks